How to Bewitch a Wolf

SCHOLASTIC

Scholastic Children's Books
An imprint of Scholastic Ltd
Euston House, 24 Eversholt Street, London, NW1 1DB, UK
Registered office: Westfield Road, Southam, Warwickshire, CV47 0RA

First published in the UK by Scholastic Ltd, 2017

ISBN 978 1407 16252 2

A CIP catalogue record for this book
is available from the British Library.

Printed by CPI Group (UK) Ltd, Croydon, CR0 4YY
Papers used by Scholastic Children's Books are made
from wood grown in sustainable forests.

1 3 5 7 9 10 8 6 4 2

www.scholastic.co.uk

For K&E and for Tabitha Heaton

Chapter One

The Witch's Way

"Again!" commanded the witch. She stamped her foot, and the ragged hem of her black dress swished across the muddy earth.

"Again? Really?" Charlie wriggled to find a more comfy position. It was getting chilly out here in the woods. The autumn leaves were scratchy under her jeans and her legs were starting to cramp.

"It's cold," her friend Kat grumbled opposite her. With her eyes closed, Charlie made a sympathetic face in response.

The witch sighed. "All right. Let's stop for a bit. Come back in and we'll have tea." She turned on the heel of her black boot and opened the door of her tumbledown cottage.

Charlie let out a breath in relief. She opened her eyes to find Kat grinning.

"Thought she'd never give us a rest!" Kat's eyes flashed bright green under her huge glasses.

"I kn-know! We've been out here for hours!" Charlie shook out her aching limbs and turned her face to the weak sun.

Agatha was a hard taskmaster. For the last seven months the witch had been pushing Charlie and Kat further and further, helping them to develop their magical powers. It wasn't easy. Spells took a lot of practice. And there was so much to learn.

Charlie scribbled a quick note in the lever-arch file next to her:

Wear warmer clothes for telepathy lessons.

The file was now so full of information it needed coloured dividers for all the sections. Charlie flipped the pages back to the start, feeling the heavy weight of her work – all that writing! She'd even had to make a contents page to organize it. She ran her finger over the biro indents:

Herbs:
- Healing
- Luck
- Protection
- Energy
- Love/Friendship
- Sleep

Crystals:
- Healing
- Prophecy
- Communication
- Calming

Charlie stopped her finger at:

Moon Phases:
- New
- Waxing
- Full
- Waning
- Eclipse

She felt a thrill run down her spine. There was due to be a lunar eclipse in three weeks' time. Everyone in town was talking about it. What's more, it would be on the thirty-first of October: Halloween (or "Samhain", as Agatha called it).

Samhain marked the end of summer and the start of the colder, harder months. It was an important night for witches. Traditionally, the Samhain blessing they chanted brought luck and strength to the village to see the people through the winter ahead. In Broomwood, Charlie's village, no one had done the blessing for seventeen years – not since Agatha had given up magic. The winters that followed had felt long and harsh. Some of the houses had been flooded at Christmastime three years in a row.

This year, Charlie was determined things would be different. Agatha had said that, if they were ready, Charlie and Kat could do the Samhain ritual themselves! Charlie grinned to herself – she couldn't wait. When a lunar eclipse fell, when the moon was dark, witchcraft was at its most powerful. Their magic would be extra strong. Or, as Charlie had put it in the note she'd made at the time:

Eclipse + Samhain = Something special

Three weeks to go... Then Charlie and Kat would do their first blessing! Maybe it would bring the village good luck.

A low buzzing ran through Charlie's bones at the thought of it, making her squirm.

"Woah!" cried Kat. "You're glowing so brightly!" She shielded her eyes with her hand.

"Sorry!" laughed Charlie. "I was just th-thinking about Halloween."

"Well stop it or I'll have to get prescription sunglasses."

Kat sensed magic by light. To her, Agatha and Charlie had a soft glow. Whenever the two witches were doing a spell, the glow became stronger. For Charlie, magic felt like the warm fizz of an electrical current. She forced her mind away from Halloween and the buzzing in her bones eased.

"Tea's ready!" called Agatha from the cottage.

Kat sprang to her feet. She held out her hand to pull Charlie up and, as they touched, Charlie felt the hum of connection between them. Charlie was a new witch and Kat was her familiar. Familiars were usually animals: toads or crows, or cats. But Kat was a *human* familiar, and together, Agatha had told them, Charlie and Kat could be very powerful.

Charlie pushed open the door of Agatha's old cottage. The air was steamy and a pot of water bubbled on the fire. Charlie ducked under a hanging crystal and plonked herself on the rug by the flames. She rubbed her hands to warm them and Agatha passed her a mug of hot tea. Charlie bent her head and breathed in the steam; it smelled sweet and floral. She looked up to find Agatha raising her eyebrows in a silent question.

"OK," Charlie sighed. She sniffed the tea. "Um... I can smell h-h-honey..." She sniffed again. "Camomile, lavender..." She screwed up her face to try and identify the other herbs. There was something sharper there too... "N-nettle?" she tried.

Agatha gave a little nod.

Phew. Little nods counted as high praise from Agatha.

"For energy," Agatha explained as she gave Kat a mug of her own.

Charlie nursed the hot mug in her hands, warming her fingers. She took a little sip and shivered with pleasure as the liquid ran through her.

Kat looked at her watch. "Whoops! It's five – I have to be getting home soon," she said. "Mum'll be back from work in an hour." Kat's mum worked shifts at the local supermarket.

Five p.m.! Charlie was shocked too. Where had the day gone? Oh yes: mainly in sitting on the cold ground, failing at telepathy. She rubbed the base of her back.

"Do you think we'll ever be able to see into each other's heads?"

"Absolutely," answered Agatha firmly. "You just have to focus."

"I am f-f-focusing," muttered Charlie defensively. She blushed as she felt her stammer flare up.

"No – you're *thinking*. I can tell." Agatha pursed her mouth. "It's not something you can force, Charlie. You have to *feel* it." Agatha put her gloved hand on the top of Charlie's head. A warm tingle ran across her scalp.

"Relax your body." Agatha's voice became low and soft. "Concentrate on your breathing. Feel the air flowing into your lungs and out again. Let your mind go."

Charlie could hear the gentle crackle of the fire; she

felt the warmth of the rug under her legs. Her limbs softened and her head dropped under Agatha's hand.

"Try to keep your thoughts still," said the witch softly. "Focus on one thing."

Charlie felt sleepy. She pictured her nice warm bed, her duvet pulled up tight to her shoulders and her pouch of lucky heather swinging over her head, back and forth, back and forth. She could smell a sweet, woody fragrance and a memory popped into her mind. All at once she was back there, on the moonlit heath. A little white plant sparkled brightly before her and Hopfoot the crow was cawing in her ear as she snipped a flower.

Kat cried out and Charlie opened her eyes.

"I saw it! Just for a second, but I saw it!" Kat was nodding in excitement, her glasses jiggling up and down wildly on her nose. "You were on open land somewhere, and there was a white flower."

Charlie's face broke into a wide grin, "I was p-picking heather!" she said. She looked at Agatha, her eyes bright.

Agatha nodded as she took her hand away from Charlie's head.

*

"I'm home!" Charlie's voice rang out in the hallway. She heard a muffled response from the top of the house, and made her way up the teeny cottage stairs to see Mum poking her head down from a hatch in the ceiling.

"We're clearing out the loft," Mum announced. There was a tinkle of metal and she pulled her head back up for a moment. "No, Annie! Put that down," she yelled to Charlie's little sister. Then she was back. "There's all kinds of junk up here. It's a real mess – Annie's having a great time. Come and see!"

Charlie put a foot on the ladder to climb up, and felt a shiver of electricity run through her. The family had inherited their house from a distant relative of Mum's, Great-Aunt Bess. Mum and Dad loved the old cottage, with its wonky stairs and ancient stone walls. They had no idea that, when Bess was alive:

1. She was sometimes known as Eliza.
2. She was a friend of Agatha's, and, most importantly. . .
3. She was a witch.

Not only a witch, but a witch who had got herself tangled in some very dark magic. Charlie frowned. She hoped there wasn't anything too dangerous hiding up there in the loft.

Charlie pulled herself up on to the old dusty floor and gazed around. Wow. Mum wasn't joking – the attic *was* a mess! There were stacks of old saucepans, and bundles of fabric. Ancient leather suitcases were piled in the corner with cracked plates teetering precariously on top of them, and, under the eaves, an armchair lay on its side, with its springs popping out. Annie was jumping up and down on a worn out sofa cushion, sending up puffs of dust into the air with a "Wheee!"

Mum was twirling around in an old hat and a set of pearls.

"Ta-da!" she said, waving her arms high. "I found a whole box of clothes and scarves. Some of them are gorgeous!"

"What's it all doing up here?"

"Everything Bess owned got stored up here in case we wanted it." Mum waved her hand around the space. "I think most of it is rubbish but there could be a few pieces of interest. Dad might know."

Charlie's dad was working on a big restoration project out at Broom Hill on the edge of town. He was becoming an expert in old property and possessions. Every now and then he came home raving about a bit of ancient kitchen equipment or jewellery he'd dug up and handed in to Broomwood Museum.

Charlie sifted through some of the wooden crates. There didn't seem to be anything witch-like. There were no potions or bottles or jars of herbs. Agatha had said Eliza (or, as the family called her, Great-Aunt Bess) had become very strange in the years before she died; she'd found an old grimoire – a book of dark magic called the Book of Shadows – and had grown obsessed with dark magic, which ended in disaster. Charlie's eyes flicked around the room but could see nothing ominous. Eliza must have either got rid of anything magic-related before she died, or else she had kept it all somewhere else.

Idly Charlie opened another wooden crate and she felt the blood rush in her ears as her pulse quickened. Her fingers prickled and her scalp started to tingle. She had spoken too soon; there *was* something magical here! Charlie glanced at Mum –

who was busy trying to rescue Annie from the pile of dusty sheets she'd wrapped herself in – and then eased her fingers down into the crate. The tingling was coming from something at the bottom. It was tugging at her attention, calling her hand down to find it. Her fingers closed around something cold and hard. She drew it up in her fist and nervously opened her hand.

There on her palm sat a grey stone ladybird, with spots carved into its back. It was heavy and smooth, about the size of a yo-yo. A shallow split ran across the top, dividing the stone into two wings. Charlie ran her fingers along the crack. She tilted the ladybird and heard a slight rattle. She shook it and heard the sound again. There was something inside! With her back to Mum, Charlie tried to open the ladybird, first twisting it, then pushing her fingers into the narrow split. The stone refused to move. Maybe it wasn't supposed to open? Maybe it was sealed fast? *No.* There was something special about this stone, Charlie was sure – something inside it. She just needed longer to figure it out. She squeezed it into the back pocket of her jeans.

"I'm going back d-down," she said, with her feet

on the ladder. "I need to get my things r-ready for school tomorrow."

"Oh cripes! It's getting late! I hadn't noticed," cried Mum. She pulled off the hat. "And Annie, you're filthy!" Clouds of grey puffed out of Annie's clothes. Annie grinned proudly as if this was the best news ever. "I didn't realize the time! I haven't even started cooking!"

"Don't worry!" Dad appeared from downstairs. "I'm home now and I've got the dinner on."

"Thanks, love," said Mum. "Here, Charlie, you take Annie." She handed the little girl down and then followed, a box of old scarves on her hip.

As they stared at each other in the hallway Charlie had to laugh. Annie wasn't the only one messy from the attic. Mum had a cobweb in her hair and a streak of something greyish across her cheek.

"Go and have a sh-shower, Mum," said Charlie. "I'll put Annie in the bath."

Mum gave her a dusty kiss.

"Come on, Annie," Charlie said, jiggling her sister on her hip. "Let's get you cleaned up."

"Bubbles?" Annie's voice was hopeful.

"Of course! We can p-pop them together." Charlie

put one finger in her cheek and pulled it out. *Pop!* Annie laughed.

"Again! Again!"

"You'll be sorry you started that trick," Mum groaned as she headed towards her shower room. "She'll make you do it over and over."

"Again! Again!"

That night in her room, Charlie sat at her desk, turning the stone ladybird around in her hands. She shook it and heard the rattle.

"What are you hiding?" Charlie whispered.

A gust of wind blew in through Charlie's open window and her papers flew across the desk. Charlie jumped up to rescue them. She closed her window and put the ladybird down as a paperweight.

There it sat on her desk, silently waiting.

Chapter Two

Bubble, Bubble

The mystery of the ladybird was still buzzing around in Charlie's head as Mum gave her and Matt a lift to school the next morning.

"I've got rehearsal at the end of the day," Matt reminded Mum, as they climbed out of the car, "so I'll be home late." Charlie's brother was in the school production of *Macbeth*. He was playing one of the witches.

"I'll be late as well," Charlie added. "I'm hanging out with Kat." It wasn't a total lie. She *would* be with Kat; it's just that Agatha would be there too, and they would be practising magic. "Have a good d-day at work," she said, waving goodbye to Mum.

"Bye, Annie!" Matt blew her a kiss. "Have fun at nursery!"

Kat was waiting for Charlie in their usual spot, just outside the school entrance. Today she wore bright stripy green and pink tights. Charlie grinned and shook her head. Kat was always in trouble for breaking the school uniform rules but she didn't seem to care. She did her lunchtime detentions quite cheerfully and continued to wear her crazy tights.

"How are you?" she asked. "Anything exciting happen last night?"

"Actually, it d-did. I found something c-cool!" Charlie dropped her voice to a whisper as Matt walked past them into school. "It belonged to Eliza – I found it in the attic – and there's something m-m-magic about it, I can tell!"

Kat's eyes widened.

"I know!" Charlie said. "It c-could be really exciting!" It took her a second to realize that Kat wasn't paying her any attention at all. Instead, she was staring at something behind Charlie.

Charlie turned around.

An older boy was riding one-handed down the

drive, standing upright on the side of his bike with both feet on the same pedal. He had a wide grin on his face, and a silver earring glinted from one ear. His hair flopped over his eyes and he lifted his free hand casually to sweep it back. The bike leaned as he looped lazily from one side of the drive to the other.

A Year 13 girl with spiky hair was riding just ahead of him, heading for the last space on the bike rack. The boy narrowed his eyes, flung his right leg over the bike seat and pedalled hard straight towards it. With a screech of his brakes, he swooped into the final bike slot just in front of Spiky.

"Hey!" she looked up. "That was my space."

"Sorry," said the boy flippantly, in a broad Northern accent. "I got here first." He locked up his bike and strolled passed Charlie and Kat into the school office.

"Who is *that*?" Kat turned to Charlie.

"I don't know," said Charlie irritably. "He m-must be new... Did you hear w-what I was saying before?"

"Oh. Sorry. What?" Kat said.

"Never m-m-mind," mumbled Charlie as they walked through the entrance.

The boy was just ahead of them, approaching the reception office. He knocked on the side of the glass hatch. "Zak Crawford, Year 9," he drawled.

"Hello!" Mrs Fisher in the school office gave him a welcoming smile. "If you wait on the sofa for a moment, a buddy from your year will come to collect you."

"What?" said Zak. "I don't need a *buddy*." He emphasized the word as if it was the stupidest thing in the world.

Charlie walked on past Zak towards the double doors that led to the hallway. She turned to roll her eyes at Kat but her friend wasn't there. Charlie looked back to see Kat pretending to tie her shoelace, just by the new boy.

Mrs Fisher was still explaining the merits of the buddy system to Zak: "They'll help you find your way around, introduce you to friends. . ."

"I don't think I'll need help making friends," Zak sneered. "I'll just try my luck. Without a *buddy*."

"Wait!" Mrs Fisher called after him. "Hang on. . .

There are some papers . . . . ah. . ." She leaned out of the hatch but he ignored her and strode past Charlie to the double doors, marching through them and not caring that they swung back and nearly hit her.

"Nice," said Charlie sarcastically.

"Yep," said Kat as she caught up. "I'm glad I stayed to check him out. At least we know what he's like now. He might be cute, but he's not likely to make friends with that attitude." She waved to Charlie as the bell rang. "See you for lunch later."

By lunchtime it was clear that Charlie and Kat weren't the only ones to find Zak annoying. According to school gossip, in PE he'd refused to pass the football even once, in music he'd carried on a long drum solo, drowning out the guitar riff Toby had been practising for ages, and in art he'd sniggered at Katie's self-portrait.

He was certainly causing a stir. Throughout the morning Charlie had heard rumour after rumour:

Zak had been expelled from his last school.

His parents had sent him away to live with his grandparents.

He was mean.

He was a show-off.

His trouser legs were too short.

He was Bad News.

In the canteen, Charlie took her tray and joined Kat at their favourite table.

"Water?" Kat said, holding up a jug.

Charlie nodded. Kat poured it into Charlie's glass. Just as she lifted it to her lips, Charlie caught a sharp smell, like vinegar.

"Ew." She wrinkled her nose and put her glass down again.

"What?" Kat looked puzzled. She took a swig of her own water. "It's fine!" she said, shrugging. "It's just water."

Charlie sniffed hers again and pushed it aside. It smelt awful – the school must be using some new filter. No one else seemed bothered – all around her children were gulping it down – but just the smell of it made her retch. She made a mental note to bring in her own water bottle from now on.

"Don't look," Kat said in a whisper. Charlie looked. Zak had walked in.

"I said *don't* look!"

"Sorry!" Charlie looked back down.

Kat's green eyes followed Zak.

"You know," she said, as she sipped her water, "maybe we're being a bit harsh. Maybe he's just nervous." She took another sip. "He seems quite nice, actually."

"You've never even sp-spoken to him," said Charlie dismissively.

"No, but there's something about him. . . I can't put my finger on it. . ."

Charlie felt a little shiver of jealousy run through her as she watched her friend gazing across the canteen, her eyes fixed on the new boy.

It wasn't just Kat who seemed to be warming to Zak. At the end of school that day a handful of students had gathered by his locker.

"Hey, nice ball work in PE." Kevin Anders high-fived him.

"Cool drums, man." Toby gave Zak a nod of appreciation.

Charlie kept walking. There was no way she was giving Zak any attention.

"*Wa-ha-ha-ha!*"

She heard a loud cackle from the school hall and poked her head through the doorway. The rehearsal for *Macbeth* was in full swing. Charlie saw Matt standing in a group of three.

"When shall we three meet again?" one actor read from her script.

"You need to sound more witch-like, Janine," came Miss Knevitt's voice from the director's chair. "Witches are old hags."

Charlie bit back a smile.

Janine hunched her back. She scowled and made her voice shaky:

"When shall we three meet again?" she rasped, sounding like a strangled cat.

"Perfect!" cried Miss Knevitt. "You sound *exactly* right. Just like a witch."

To Charlie's amazement, over the next few days, Zak somehow became more and more popular. To Charlie it seemed he was no less annoying, no less arrogant, no less Bad News. But it soon became clear that the rest of the school saw things differently. In fact, Charlie mused, the week had gone a bit like this:

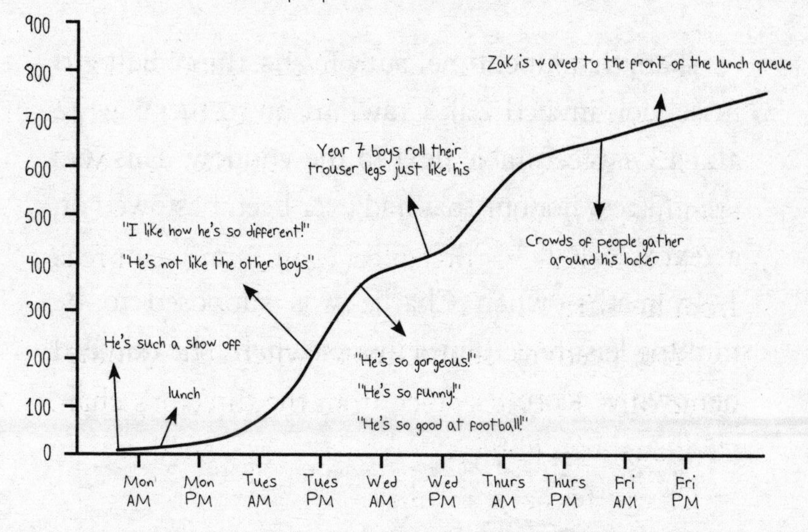

Even Kat had taken to lingering for longer and longer periods of time by the school exit. Every day Charlie felt like she was practically *dragging* her friend to Agatha's.

"Just a minute," Kat would say, adjusting her glasses casually as she scanned every student leaving. "You start. I'll catch you up!"

And every day Charlie would head off on her own.

By Friday morning, in the eyes of the school, Zak had turned into some kind of mini-god and Kat could talk about nothing else. Charlie was completely fed up.

Then, that lunchtime, Suzy Evans, the coolest girl in school, invited Zak Crawford on to the Year 12 and 13 canteen table next to the window. This was the greatest honour that had ever been bestowed on a Year 9.

In maths, when Charlie was supposed to be ranking leisure activities in a pie chart, she doodled her own version:

That Friday afternoon, on the way to Agatha's, Kat was *still* talking about Zak. She bounced through the woods, chattering away:

"Did you notice he has a little scar just by his mouth? I wonder how he got that."

Charlie shrugged in answer as she snapped a skinny branch off a nearby bush and broke it apart in her fingers. Kat was *her* friend. Her only friend, if she was honest. And they were supposed to be a team, just the two of them.

There was a loud *Caw!* from a treetop and a crow swooped down. "Oh, hi, Hopfoot!" said Kat happily as he perched on her shoulder. She tickled the top of his head and he ruffled his feathers against her.

"Hi," said Charlie, but Hopfoot ignored her and cuddled into Kat's neck.

Grumpily, Charlie left them behind and pushed through the bushes to find the narrow path to Agatha's house. There was a fine drizzle in the air and the branches pinged back against her, showering little splashes on to her face. In frustration Charlie shoved one bush hard and scratched her hand on a bramble. She stomped into the cottage.

"Who put a curse in your bonnet?" the witch asked as Charlie slumped down in an armchair. Agatha raised her eyebrows but Charlie shook her head. She didn't want to talk about it.

Kat came in, Hopfoot on her shoulder.

"I think someone's hungry," she laughed as the

crow nibbled the ends of her short red hair. "Ow! Hopfoot! Leave some hair for me!"

Agatha handed her some nuts and Hopfoot happily munched them out of Kat's palm.

"Right," the old witch began, "we've got just over two weeks until Samhain and, if you're going to do the blessing together, there's still a lot of work to do." Charlie winced. Despite trying every day, they hadn't managed to repeat their telepathy skills of last Sunday night.

Charlie took her place on the rug opposite Kat and crossed her legs under her knees.

"Now," said Agatha, "empty your minds. Focus on your breathing. Slow down. Feel the air flow in and out. . ."

There was an itch on Charlie's neck. One of her curls was caught under her collar and it tickled against her skin. Should she brush it away? If she did then Agatha would know she wasn't concentrating. But if she didn't it was going to annoy her. Would that be worse? Maybe, if Agatha wasn't watching, she could sneak her hand up. She opened her eyes a tiny bit. All she could see was the old rug on the floor. Her face was still wet from the drizzle and her jumper felt heavy and damp on her shoulders. She shifted slightly to ease the itch.

"Stop," said Agatha, and Charlie opened her eyes. The witch was looking at her closely.

"S-s-sorry," Charlie mumbled. She pulled her hair out of her shirt collar.

Kat blinked and yawned. She looked like she was waking from a trance. At least one of them had got it right.

"Let's try something else for now," said Agatha. She lifted a pile of long thin twigs. "You can help me make a blessing wreath for the new year."

"New year?"

"Yes. Samhain – what you call Halloween. The new year."

Charlie looked at Kat, confused. Surely New Year was January the first? Kat shrugged in answer.

"January isn't the new year for witches," said Agatha quickly, as if she'd read Charlie's thoughts. "Our calendar starts on the first of November. Remember I told you Samhain marks the end of the harvest and the start of the cold weather? That's why we do the blessing then, on the night of the thirty-first of October. We give thanks for the old year past, and we wish for peace for the new year to come." She lifted the twigs on to her lap and began to plait. Her gloved fingers moved quickly over and under and soon she had the start of a circular shape.

Charlie curled her feet to the side and picked up some twigs of her own. They were thin and bendy – they looked like they were made from an old vine.

"Honeysuckle," said Agatha in answer to Charlie's unasked question. "It aids friendship," she added quickly and reached for another twig. Charlie sneaked a glance at Kat, but her friend was absorbed in her task, weaving the twigs in and out.

Charlie looked down. There was silence for a while. Charlie concentrated on plaiting. After a time, Agatha spoke again.

"Eliza and I used to make these together," she said. "We sat right here, by the fire, years ago." The witch reached for another twig and paused a moment before she plaited it in. "Eliza loved Samhain!" she said with a little smile. "She would write a new blessing chant every year for us to say."

"Can witches write their own sp-spells?" Charlie was surprised. She'd only ever used spells written down in Agatha's old grimoire.

"Some can," said Agatha. "Not all. Eliza could. At Samhain I'd walk over to her house. We'd stand together before the old Akelarre, where our sisters had stood for years and years before us. We lit the fire and waited till midnight to see the new year in. We hung our wreaths and we chanted Eliza's spell together in the early hours of the new day, bringing luck and strength to the village to see it through the winter."

Charlie stared at Agatha. She knew where the old Akelarre was – it was the big ancient fireplace in their lounge. Nowadays it had a modern mantelpiece with family photos and a pot plant sitting on it. But still it tingled with the ghost of magic past.

"It's up to you what you put in your wreath," Agatha was saying. "You could put a sigil, like a pentagram . . ."

Charlie turned to her lever-arch file and found:

Sigils:

- Pentagram
- Pentacle
- Baphomet
- Endless Knot
- All-Seeing Eye

". . . or just herbs that you like. Focus on what you want for the village in the winter to come. Think about the people, the weather, the crops. Your wreath is personal too, so you can add in a wish for yourself – a goal you want to achieve in the next few months."

Charlie swallowed. She knew what she wanted. She wanted her best friend – her familiar – to be all hers again. She glanced sideways at Kat and turned to her page on herbs. There were herbs for encouraging friendship, for love, but nothing for bonding someone to you.

"I'm just going out to gather some more honeysuckle," said Kat. She closed the cottage door behind her.

"Um," Charlie began quickly, "what herb could I use to link s-s-s-someone to me? I mean, o-o-only to me?"

Agatha put down her wreath and gave Charlie a questioning glance. "Possession?" she said. "That's dark magic, Charlie." She shook her head slightly. "It's wrong to *make* someone like you or pay attention to you. And even if you bound someone to you by force, it would be meaningless. It is not real if it has to be forced."

Charlie looked away. Her throat was tight.

"I-I have to go," she said. "It's nearly d-d-dinner time. C-can you say goodbye to K-K-Kat for me?"

"OK, Charlie," said Agatha softly. She passed Charlie a twig of honeysuckle. "Hang this over your bed tonight," she said. "I think it'll help."

Chapter Three

Bewitched

That night, Charlie tossed and turned. She didn't think she could face another week of Kat practically ignoring her. She couldn't bear the dreamy look Kat always had on her face these days, or the way she kept looking over Charlie's shoulder, as if she wanted to be somewhere else. It hurt.

Charlie hadn't even had a chance to tell her about the stone ladybird. She still didn't know what it was, but it definitely used to be Eliza's; she could sense it. Maybe she could ask Agatha sometime when Kat wasn't there.

No! Charlie stopped herself. This was getting stupid! Kat was her friend. She shifted in bed and, in the dim light, caught sight of the honeysuckle hanging on her bedstead. Friendship – that's what Agatha said it was for. Charlie closed her eyes and focused her breathing the way Agatha had taught her. She pictured Kat, bouncing around in her usual excited way, wearing her mad tights and enormous glasses. Charlie smiled. Kat was her familiar – Agatha had said so. They had a special bond and there was no way Charlie would let anything break it.

The next morning Charlie felt much better. So what if Kat had a little crush on a boy? Today she and Kat would get their telepathy right. She texted Kat first thing:

Can't w8 to c u @ A's this morning ☺

A second later, her phone pinged:

Charlie smiled. It was going to be OK.

She headed downstairs and helped herself to some toast.

"Ah, Charlie!" Dad strolled in wearing his old jeans. "Good. You can help me in the garden. I want to pull that ivy down. It's taking over the house."

"Sure. C-can I do it this afternoon though? I'm hanging out with Kat this m-morning."

"Yep. I have to go up to Broom Hill anyway and pick up some tools."

"How's it g-going up there?" Charlie loved hearing all about the Broom Hill project. For hundreds of years, Broomwood village had had a connection with witches and magic. There was an old pub, the Spindle, which dated back to the thirteenth century and was said to be haunted by its former witchy customers. There was a new-age shop, Moonquest, which sold all sorts of crystals and candles and incense and spells (although, as Agatha liked to remind Charlie, "*They aren't* real *spells*."). And there was the village wishing well, the oldest in England.

The history books were full of photographs of olden-day Broomwood women – women who were said to be witches. They had lived out on Broom Hill in a group of five cottages. Nowadays the cottages were in ruins. Three still had stone walls and bits of roof, but two had been completely destroyed. The council had decided to restore the better cottages, and dig up the others. There were all kinds of historians and archaeologists interested in the site, and the artefacts were being gathered up for an exhibition on the history of witchcraft in Broomwood. Of course, no one believed the women had *actually* been witches – no one except Agatha, Charlie and Kat.

Dad had found a job on the Broom Hill project and Charlie had never seen him enjoy his work so much. He was grinning as he told Charlie about the latest discovery.

"A couple of weeks ago we found the remains of an apothecary – a kind of olden-day chemist. We think that's where the 'witches'" – he made bunny ears with his fingers – "stored their healing medicines. There are all sorts of bottles and jars."

Charlie's ears pricked up. *Witch bottles and jars!*

"You can come and see, if you like," said Dad. "I'm going up there again tomorrow."

"Yes please!" said Charlie.

She waved goodbye and then opened the backdoor and set off for Agatha's, climbing over the old stone wall at the end of her garden and walking briskly through the woods. It was going to be a good day; she could feel it.

"Hey!" Kat pounced on her and took her arm.

"G-good timing," said Charlie. "You arrived just as I did!"

"Well," said Kat, "I *am* telepathic."

Charlie laughed as she pushed Agatha's door open.

The witch looked at her questioningly and Charlie nodded with a smile. Agatha seemed satisfied.

"Let's get started," said Kat. She was bouncing on her toes, keen to begin.

"Yep," said Agatha, "outside." She led the way into the garden.

Charlie sat herself down on a patch of grass and pulled her jumper tighter around her. "You think of something this time," she said as Kat sat down opposite.

"OK!"

They both closed their eyes.

Agatha's low voice began, controlling their breathing and directing their focus. Charlie felt herself lighten. Her shoulders dropped down and her head went fuzzy. It was like she was floating somewhere high. The land was spread out below her as she skimmed over the tops of the trees. Charlie felt the heat of connection with Kat, a gentle fizz of energy between them. Down, down she drifted until she was in a clearing. Hopfoot was there, dancing his little crow moves. There was something different about him. He was still a crow, but he had a funny glow, as though he was lit from within. Then Charlie realized – she was seeing him as Kat saw him! The telepathy was working!

All of a sudden, into the clearing walked a person. Charlie screwed up her face to see who it was. A boy. Tall and dark. He sauntered across the grass, whistling. Charlie screwed up her face . . . it looked like. . .

"Zak!" Charlie said out loud. She stood up. "You were th-th-thinking about Zak!" She was cross. The fact that she was probably unreasonably cross just made her even crosser.

"So?" said Kat, turning bright red. "I'm allowed to think about him! They're *my* thoughts!"

"N-n-not when you're supp-supp-supposed to be building a b-bond with me!" Charlie could feel her stutter getting worse.

"I can't help what I think about. And I'm not letting you see into my head if you're just going to complain about what you see."

"Fine!" shouted Charlie. "I d-d-d-don't even want t-t-to s-s-s-see!" Her voice had deserted her. She took a breath to try to bring it back, but there was so much pressure in her chest it refused to behave. In frustration she folded her arms and glared at Kat, letting her eyes do the talking. Kat glared back.

"Right." Agatha stood up. "I'm giving you both the weekend off," she said firmly. "Go and do something else. Be with your families, have some time by yourselves, I don't care what you get up to. But you need to come back next week with a better attitude."

All afternoon Charlie helped Dad rip down the ivy. It was hard work, but just what she needed. She pulled at the vines, venting her frustrations with every tug, every rip.

"You're doing well," Dad said as he poked his head round the corner. "Really getting into it."

Charlie grunted in response and yanked another strand down.

Stupid Zak. Stupid Kat. Stupid voice. Stupid stammer.

There was nothing more annoying than wanting to say something and being blocked by her own body! She scowled and pulled until her arms hurt.

She was working at the ivy on the side of the house, the bit opposite the old apple tree with the face in the trunk like a troll. She wrapped her arms round a particularly stubborn bit and yanked hard, leaning herself back. At last it gave way and she nearly tumbled to the ground.

There was something funny about the base of the wall left behind. Charlie bent down and parted the remaining leaves. The bricks at the bottom were grey and grimy. She knelt to see – *glass*. It was a window! She touched it and felt a familiar shiver run up her arm. Magic!

"Dad! There's a w-window here!"

"Is there?" Dad came round the corner. "So there is!" he said, wiping the glass with the bottom of his shirt. He stood back and looked up at the old cottage. "I wonder which room it's for. . ." He mumbled and began to count the various rooms that faced the garden.

"I can't work it out." He rubbed his forehead, puzzled. "It's so low it must be some kind of cellar." He shrugged. "I didn't know we had a cellar," he admitted.

He tried to prise the window open. "It's stuck fast," he said. "There's no give in the wood at all." He pushed his curly hair out of his eyes. "Maybe it'll open from the inside."

Charlie frowned. She touched the wood and a cold buzz ran up her arm. She pulled back quickly before Dad noticed.

"How do we g-get inside?" She'd never seen stairs that led down. The staircase ended on the ground floor.

"I don't know," said Dad. "Maybe there's a trapdoor in the floor somewhere. Strange that I've never seen it, though – when I did up the kitchen and the lounge last year there wasn't anything unusual in the floor of either room. Come on, let's have a look on the house plans the surveyor drew up."

Charlie and Dad spread them over the kitchen table. There was no trapdoor, no extra set of stairs, no cellar marked anywhere. Just in case, Charlie and Dad pulled up the hallway rug and they checked with a torch in the cupboard under the stairs. Dad finally admitted defeat.

"I don't think we can get to the cellar. Never mind, Charlie. It's probably just an old storeroom. These old cottages often had cellars that were sealed up long ago because they were too damp to use."

Charlie bit her lip. It was more than just an old storeroom. She knew it.

That night Charlie had a familiar dream; a dream she'd had lots of times since they'd moved to the cottage. There was chanting coming up from under the house. She saw candles in old alcoves and bottles of potions sparkling in the light of the flickering flames. In her sleep she shivered. There was something not right: this was a dark place, a hidden place. . . A place of magic. . .

Her eyes shot open. Her heart was thumping. The hidden room. It was Eliza's spell room! That was why there hadn't been any of Eliza's witchy things up in the loft; they were all hidden under the house, behind a spell-sealed window. The only question was. . .

"How do I get inside?" Charlie whispered into the darkness.

Chapter Four

I'll Huff and I'll Puff

The next day Charlie got up early. Dad was going to Broom Hill and he'd promised to show her the apothecary's cottage they'd found. Charlie was twitchy with excitement. She couldn't wait to stand on the site of an ancient witch cottage! She pulled on her old jeans with trembling fingers and headed down to the kitchen. Mum was already up, trying to persuade Annie to eat some porridge.

"Come on, Annie," she was saying. "One for Daddy, one for Mummy, one for Annie." She held out a spoon.

"No!" said Annie, and she shoved the bowl away. Mum waved her hand in defeat.

"That's n-nice." Charlie nodded to a green scarf round Mum's neck.

"Isn't it!" said Mum. She untied it and opened it out so that Charlie could see. It slipped through her fingers smoothly. "It's pure silk," she said. "I found it in the loft. It must have belonged to Bess."

"It's really pretty." Charlie leaned closer to see her great-aunt's scarf. She touched the pattern of dark green vines on the sage background. "It looks g-good on you!"

"Thanks. Are you off to see Kat?" Mum asked.

"No. N-n-not today."

Mum looked surprised. Before she could ask any more questions, Charlie hastily added:

"I'm g-g-going to Broom Hill with Dad."

"Kat coming?" Annie was looking from her mum to her big sister, confused. She loved Kat. Every time Kat came over she'd bounce Annie high in the air or swing her round and round till they were both dizzy.

"No, not today." Charlie ruffled her hair and lifted the porridge spoon. "One for K-K-Kat," she said and Annie gobbled it up.

*

In the car, on the way to Broom Hill, Charlie couldn't stop worrying away at the problem of how to get into the cellar. At last she said:

"C-c-could we cut a hole in the kitchen floor?"

"What?"

"To get to the cellar."

"Ah! And the answer is no," said Dad firmly as he took a hard left turn. "I've only just done up the kitchen!"

"We c-could smash through the window from the outside?"

"Sorry, love. I know you're curious. I am too. But I'm not destroying one of our original windows to get to a useless old cellar." He pulled on to a narrow track and they bounced up the hill slowly. Dad parked at the top and clicked the handbrake tight.

Charlie opened her door. There was mud everywhere.

"Look out," Dad warned. "It's slippery. Don't slide into a hole. And you need to wear this." He handed Charlie a bright yellow jacket and helmet.

"Really?" Charlie wrinkled her nose.

"Yep. Site rules."

Charlie groaned out loud. But Dad wouldn't be budged.

She put on the huge jacket and fitted the helmet in the car window reflection. She looked ridiculous – a bright yellow kind of ridiculous.

"This way!" said Dad cheerfully. "Watch out for witches. *Wa-ha-ha-ha*!" He cackled as he headed along a muddy track towards a large digger.

When Charlie reached him she found him standing looking down at a large triangular pit. "Is that it?"

"Yep. That's the apothecary. Funny shape to choose, isn't it?"

Charlie nodded. Why would they have built it like a triangle?

"We found five triangular plots," Dad was explaining. "They were arranged around a piece of stone in the centre of the site. It's strange. The archaeologist doesn't know why the houses were built that way either." He waved his hand over the pit below him. "This is the site of one of the supposed witch cottages that was destroyed in the 1600s. It seems this plot had a cellar. We've found some amazing things under the ground:

bottles and books and jars. That's why we think it used to be the apothecary."

Charlie closed her eyes for a moment. Her mind was flitting back to what Agatha had once told her. The witches had been a bit like village doctors, she'd said – wise women living on the hill, helping people with their problems.

Broom Hill would have been busy in those days. She could picture the women working together in their grey stone cottages, brewing up remedies and cures in pots on their fireplaces. They'd have herb gardens and crystals, just like Agatha, and there would have been a long queue of farmers wanting a potion to make their crops grow, or a salve for a blacksmith's burned hand. . .

But their way of life would turn out to be short-lived. In the mid-1600s, Matthew Hopkins had arrived: the Witchfinder General. It was his job to hunt out witches and put them on trial. Not many women survived a witch trial, Agatha had told Charlie. Many were killed, and the ones who escaped went into hiding to avoid the Witchfinder. Charlie shuddered at the thought of it. How terrifying it must have been for the witches on the hill, huddling in fear of what was to come!

Agatha had told Charlie that only a few Broom Hill witches escaped from Hopkins. They moved their meeting place, their Akelarre, out to the woods, to Charlie's house. They hid in cottages in the woods and practised witchcraft in secret. Most of the houses on the hill were vandalized by villagers, scared of the stories Hopkins had told.

"Careful here," said Dad, climbing down a wooden ladder into the triangular pit. Charlie followed. The earth felt strange at the base. Charlie shivered and wrapped her coat tighter round herself.

"We found bottles like this one," Dad was saying, holding out a little squat glass thing. Charlie took it from him and felt the tingle of magic. A cold, sharp kind of magic. Charlie frowned.

"There were pots too, and old buttons and trinkets, but they've mostly been collected up for the museum. Have a look around if you like. I'll be a while – we've started on a new site over there." Dad pointed sideways as he climbed up the ladder. "We found the remains of what we think is a wolf!"

Charlie stood in the pit all alone and closed her eyes, trying to locate what felt so strange. After a moment she sensed it: there was a funny kind of cold buzzing coming up through the mud, as though she were standing on electrical ice—

"Nice," came a voice. Charlie's eyes flew open. It was Zak – of all the people. He stood up on the surface, laughing at her. "Never seen a banana meditating before." He gestured with his head towards her bright yellow jacket and helmet. Charlie willed her voice to sound strong.

"Wh-wh-what are you d-d-doing here?" she said. *Great*. She winced. *Really strong, Charlie*.

"I . . . I . . . I," Zak said, mimicking her, "am just having fun. Or as you call it," he put on a Southern accent, "f-f-f-fun."

Charlie scowled at him.

"Hey! I'm just teasing!" Zak smiled. He slid down the ladder without touching the rungs with his feet. "Cool!" He reached out and swiped the squat bottle Dad had handed her. Charlie's eyes widened.

"That's f-f-for the mu-mu-museum," she said.

"All right. Don't get your knickers in a twist. I'm giving it to my gran." He laughed at Charlie's expression. "She works in the museum. We're collecting everything for the exhibition." Charlie tilted her head, not sure whether to believe him.

"We've got some amazing stuff so far!" Zak's eyes lit up. "Iron chests 'n' bottles 'n' books and all kinds of things." He leaned in towards Charlie. "My gran says," he said, in a pantomime whisper, "that there used to be witches on this hill. Witches with wolves!" He looked at Charlie to see if he was scaring her. Charlie shrugged casually. Zak threw back his head:

"Aroooooooo!" he howled.

"You all right, Charlie?" Dad had come over and was peering over the edge.

"Oh, hi, Mr Samuels."

"Zak! You should be wearing a helmet!"

"It's OK, Mr Samuels. I just left it over there. I'll go get it now." He gestured with his head. Dad nodded.

"How's your gran?"

"She's fine, ta."

Charlie looked from Dad to Zak.

"Tell her I've got some more bits and pieces for the collection."

"Will do!" said Zak in a super-cheery voice. "See you at school, Charlie!"

"How do you know h-h-him?" Charlie asked in the car on the way home.

"Zak? He's Martha Crawford's grandson. I know Martha from the project – she's curating the exhibition of artefacts we've found. Zak came to live with her a couple of weeks ago."

Charlie shifted in her seat. So Zak had been telling the truth about his gran then.

"Sounds like he had a hard time at his old school," Dad continued. "Got in a bit of trouble, I think." He rubbed his forehead. "Anyway, he's living here for a bit while his parents sell their house up in Sheffield. I think they're moving down later this year." Dad turned right into their road. "I hope he gets on OK at your school."

"People seem to l-l-like him," said Charlie, leaning forward to turn the radio on. She didn't want to talk about Zak Crawford any more.

At home, Charlie ate lunch in near silence, thinking through possible ways into the cellar. She was determined to find the way to the spell room. After her sandwich she spent ages slowly going over everywhere she'd already searched with Dad, just in case they'd missed something. Then she opened the back door to the garden and stood staring at the grimy glass window.

She'd brought a bucket of cleaning stuff outside with her, in hope that a clear window would help her see in. She braced herself, sprayed the window and began to rub off the grease and dirt. The electrical current of magic was so strong that she could only work slowly, resting after every wipe. It took hours! She shivered as she worked. The magic was almost painful, prickling at her bones with an icy fizz.

Charlie clicked on a torch and, cupping her hands around her eyes, pressed her face to the glass. To her surprise the torchlight just reflected back, straight into her eyes. It didn't light up the room at all. It was as though Eliza had made sure nobody could see what was going on in that cellar.

She stepped back, trying to remember everything Agatha had told her about Eliza. As well as the Book of Shadows, Eliza had found a seventeenth-century diary of an old witch. It told of the persecution of the Broom Hill witches, and of Hopkins the Witchfinder General. Eliza had become obsessed with the history of witch trials and grew angrier and angrier at how witches were treated by ordinary humans. Shortly before she died, Eliza was furious about being the only villager excluded from a christening. She'd put a curse on a baby – a girl called Suzy Evans. Her curse said Suzy would lose her singing voice at the end of her sixteenth year. It was thanks to Charlie and Kat that the curse had been defeated.

Charlie frowned. Eliza had become paranoid and secretive. She would have wanted a hidden way in. She would have wanted to protect her spell room from prying eyes.

Back at the kitchen table, Charlie made a list of possible locations for secret staircases.

A trapdoor in the floor
Behind the fireplace – the Akelarre.
May have a secret door?
Back of a wardrobe – like Narnia
Back of a bookshelf – like Anne Frank

She headed into the lounge, past Matt on his Xbox, and went straight to the fireplace. It was all smart and modern, with a new mantelpiece. She felt around the inside bricks behind the hearth and poked her head up to look through the chimney.

"What on earth are you doing?" Matt asked. "Are you expecting Santa to come early or something?"

"Um … no." Charlie yanked her head out as quickly as she could and left the room before Matt could ask her any more questions. Sitting at the kitchen table she crossed off:

~~Behind the fireplace~~

"We'll need that space for dinner, love," Mum's voice broke in. "Can you set the table?"

Charlie got out the pasta bowls. She'd have to think about it later.

Dinner was a noisy affair. Everyone was chatting about the week to come. Mum was going to be busy at the hospital, she said. She had to work an extra shift every night.

"I can pick up Annie from nursery on Monday but not for the rest of the week."

"I can do Thursday," Dad suggested. "Charlie? Matt? Can you help?"

"I've got rehearsal Tuesday and Wednesday," said Matt. "But I could pick her up on Friday." He turned to his sister. "Shall we go to the playground? I'll push you on the swings!"

Annie grinned.

"Not so high this time, Matt," said Mum, and Annie's face fell a bit.

"I'll pick you up T-T-Tuesday and Wednesday," Charlie told Annie. "We can make your Halloween costume." Even though Halloween was two weeks away, Annie was already really excited.

"What do you want to go as, Annie?" Dad asked.

"Annie be a cat!" said Annie firmly. "Like Kat."

Of course.

Charlie took her notebook up to her room and sat on her bed. She glanced around her bedroom walls, her eyes scanning every inch of plaster for a secret door. There didn't seem to be anything unusual.

She'd always been able to sense a funny, electrical tingle in her bedroom. When they'd first moved into the house, last year, the tingle had been really strong. It had felt like a fast current running through her bones. In time she had learned to recognize it for what it was: magic. Now she was used to it she didn't notice it so much.

Charlie closed her eyes and tried to focus in on it. She crossed her legs under her knees and opened her mind. There – now she was paying attention, she could feel it. It buzzed up, from the very fabric of the house, into her blood, fizzing as it passed through her. She tried to catch it – to hold on to its tail as it darted and danced. She concentrated hard, letting go of the world she knew and plunging headlong after the feeling of power. Colour blossomed and she could see the force whipping and twisting. It wanted to go to the side of her room and Charlie followed it inside her head. As it hovered over the fireplace, a surge of power pulsated, brighter and brighter, and then:

Whoosh!

It shot through the grate of her fireplace and down.

Charlie opened her eyes.

Her fireplace. She'd thought of the lounge fireplace, the meeting point the witches called the Akelarre, but not her own.

Her fingers searched the back of the dusty chimney, feeling for a catch or a break in the brickwork. Nothing. She pulled the cold grate aside and gasped.

There in the stone was the faint outline of a trapdoor. Charlie could see its edges cut into the grey slab. At one side was a lock. Charlie tried to push her fingers into the gap, desperate to prise open the door. The stone wouldn't budge. She needed the key.

She fell back on her heels in frustration. The lock was quite small, so the key must be too, wherever it was. Still, at least it was progress – she had found the door. Now she just had to find the key. She traced her fingers one last time over the outline of the trapdoor. Somewhere under it was the entrance to Eliza's spell room, Charlie was sure. She couldn't wait to see where her great-aunt had practised her witchcraft.

As she drifted off that night, it was to visions of potion bottles and herbs and jars. Charlie shivered in her sleep, buzzing with the tingle of magic that ran through her dreams.

Chapter Five

Hocus Pocus

Charlie stood by herself at the entrance to school on Monday morning. It was where she usually met Kat. But Kat wasn't there. Charlie waited a few extra minutes after the bell rang just in case, but she didn't come. Part of Charlie was relieved. They hadn't spoken since their row on Saturday and Charlie was still really cross about Kat's betrayal. How could she have brought that boy into their shared telepathy? But Charlie still missed her. She wanted her friend – wanted to tell her all about seeing Zak at Broom Hill, the magic ladybird and the hunt for Eliza's spell room. Charlie set off for maths feeling like there was something heavy pulling at the base of her stomach.

At lunch, she headed for the canteen. She scanned the huge room full of people eating with their friends. Charlie found an empty table and sat down to wait for Kat.

"Hey!" came a cross voice. "Who finished all the water?" Charlie looked up to see a girl with yellow hairclips at the next table. She was angrily shaking the empty jug at her friends.

"You snooze, you lose," was the reply from a boy.

"That's not fair!" Hairclips' voice was getting louder.

"Here" – Charlie stood up – "you c-can have this one." She passed the full water jug over, her heart beating fast from speaking to so many people at once.

"Thanks!" Hairclips gave her an enormous smile. Weird. It was only water. Water that tasted like vinegar. Charlie had been avoiding it for the last week. But, at the next table, people were carefully sharing it out as if it were liquid gold.

She sat back down. Where was Kat?

"Anyone seen Zak?" the girl at the next table said. "I wanted to invite him to my party on Saturday."

"I've already invited him to mine," said someone else quickly. "I'm sure he's coming."

Charlie shook her head in despair. Over the last

week "Zak fever" had grown. The Year 8 girls had printed out photos of him and stuck them inside their lockers. The Year 7 boys queued up to carry his books or hold his bag. And the Year 13s even let Zak into their common room from time to time.

Charlie waited and waited. But it was soon clear: Kat wasn't coming to the canteen. Nor was Mr Popular; he wasn't even on the Year 12 and 13 table. Charlie had an irrational thought: were they together somewhere? Suddenly Charlie wasn't hungry. She fled to the library. It felt like old times – the days before she'd met Kat. Back then Charlie had scurried from lesson to lesson, her head down to avoid having to speak to people. It had been Kat who had rescued her – she'd spoken to Charlie, really listened to her.

Now, six months later, back on her own in the library, Charlie felt a cold chill. She hurried down an aisle, pretending she was there to do important work, rather than to hide herself away. A narrow book caught her eye and made her stop. The book was thin, with a hard black cover. On its spine, in white writing, was: *The Broomwood Wolf and Other Myths and Legends*. Charlie drew it out. She flicked through the pages and stopped at one passage:

By the 1600s wolves were rarely seen in the UK, limited to the wilder parts of Derbyshire, Lancashire and Yorkshire. However, there were some extraordinary exceptions: namely the famous Broomwood Wolf. In January 1602, records show reports of wolf sightings in Broomwood Village, in the vicinity of Broom Hill. The reports were mixed, with some villagers describing a large white beast, others talking of hearing howling at night.

Charlie turned the page to see a full-spread drawing of the wolf. The artist had sketched it in pouncing mode, coming right at the reader, with its ears drawn back and its enormous teeth bared in a snarl. Its eyes were huge, staring out of the paper straight into Charlie. She shuddered and quickly turned the page.

A bounty was placed on the wolf. Search parties set out to hunt it down, armed with arrows, spears and knives. The beast was eventually captured and killed. The remains were buried on Broom Hill but have never been found.

The Broomwood Wolf. . . That could be the wolf bones Dad found! In a rush of excitement, Charlie checked the book out of the library to show him.

In between afternoon classes, Charlie looked for Kat. She tried by Zak's locker, but the crowds were too big to spot a small girl, even one with red hair. She tried the music rooms and the art room. She even walked past the Year 12 and 13 common room, just in case Kat was hovering outside it along with Zak's other fans.

Spiky rushed past her and opened the door of the common room.

"You're not allowed in here!" she reminded Charlie crossly, and slammed the door closed. Then she opened it a second later.

"Have you seen Zak?" she asked. "If you do, tell him Suzy says he can come in."

By the time Charlie reached Agatha's cottage that afternoon, Charlie had gone the whole school day without seeing her friend once.

As she approached, Charlie could hear Agatha laughing inside. *Agatha laughing??* Charlie frowned. She'd never heard Agatha laugh before; at least, Charlie had never made her laugh. Charlie felt suddenly shy as she pushed the cottage door open, as if she was intruding.

"Hi, Charlie." Agatha looked up, still chuckling.

"Hi," Charlie said. Out of the corner of her eye she could see Kat sitting on the rug, Hopfoot perched on her shoulder. Ah. Kat. That's who was making Agatha laugh. Kat was looking down, playing with a tassel on the rug.

"I was just about to tell Kat about scrying," Agatha said.

Charlie got out her file, ready to make notes.

"Oh, don't worry about taking notes – it's not relevant for you," said Agatha. "It's just for Kat."

"OK," said Charlie in a small voice.

She stood back and listened while Agatha explained it to Kat.

"I've never been able to scry myself," said Agatha. "Magical people are usually good at one branch of magic or another. For me it was making potions – that was always my thing. With Eliza, it was spell casting and chants. But my mother was a scryer; that means she could see into the past and future."

Charlie couldn't help herself; she inched forward in excitement.

"She couldn't see everything, just visions – brief snippets that might mean something for the past or future. There's a real art to it. Not only do you have to be able to *see* something, you have to be able to *interpret* it too."

Agatha turned to the table behind her and slowly drew back a soft piece of red velvet, faded and tatty with age.

"This was my mother's," she said. "And it was *her* mother's before her, and *her* mother's before *her*, going all the way back to the 1600s."

Charlie and Kat drew closer to see.

"Long ago, my sister-in-time lived on Broom Hill. She was a good witch, a white witch. She helped villagers and crops and animals. But the Witchfinder General didn't care how helpful witches were. He hunted any witch, and destroyed them. When he came for her, she ran from her house in the middle of the night, carrying nothing but a small bag. In it was this scrying mirror."

Agatha finished unwrapping the old velvet. There on the table lay an oval hand mirror, made of a simple wood frame, and shiny black stone.

"Obsidian," said Agatha to their unasked question. "It's a kind of volcanic glass."

Charlie frowned as she peered closer. The surface of the mirror was solid black. How was Kat supposed to see anything through there? Round the edge of the wood were rough carvings of birds.

"The crow," said Agatha. "The crow sigil runs strong in our family." Hopfoot jumped off Kat's shoulder and on to Agatha's as the witch touched one of the tiny carved wings. "Rumour has it my great-great-grandmother was a shape-shifter – she could turn into an animal!" She smiled and shook her head. "But that's another story."

Charlie stared, open-mouthed.

Agatha lifted the scrying mirror and gently placed it in Kat's hands. "Why don't you have a go?" she said.

Charlie stepped back, making space for Kat on the floor. The witch bent down, showing Kat how to set up the mirror on the ground before her. Charlie could feel her throat tighten as she watched the two of them working closely together.

"Close the curtains, Charlie," Agatha commanded over her shoulder without turning round.

Charlie pulled the heavy fabric and the room went dark. There was a *phuut* sound of a match being struck as Agatha lit a candle and placed it behind the mirror. "Close your eyes and try to centre yourself," Agatha said softly. "When you are ready, open your eyes and look into the mirror. But try not to see with your physical eyes. You want to see *through* the obsidian, into the world beyond." Kat had already closed her eyes, ready to begin.

Agatha took Charlie by the hand and led her out of the cottage. "Come," she said, "we must give Kat time."

The world was bright outside after the darkness of the cottage. Charlie blinked. There was a flutter as Hopfoot flew up to a tree branch.

Agatha sat on the stone doorstep, her feet in the grass and her face turned to the sun. After a time she spoke:

"I see great power in Kat," she said.

Charlie swallowed.

"She has a rare gift for telepathy, and, I hope, for scrying. They often go together, you know. They are both about seeing beyond the self. With time Kat will be able to see into people's heads easily, and show them what's in hers." Agatha drew up her knees, pulling the hem of her dress over them. "My mother had that gift, but it passed me by."

Charlie watched Agatha's face as she spoke. The witch closed her eyes, soaking up the sun's rays.

"She was so strong, my mother!" Agatha gave a little laugh. "She could not only connect with people, she could sense changes under the earth, feel the shift as time plotted and replotted its course. I really think, if not for her, the result of the Second World War might have been very different indeed."

"The *war*? What did she do?"

"Oh." Agatha waved her hand airily. "We witches have our uses," she said, yawning.

Charlie stared at her in amazement. She realized in a rush that she had no idea how old Agatha was. In her long dress and little black boots, the witch looked somehow other-worldly. She could have come from anywhere in time.

"Yes," Agatha was saying. "I've got no idea how to see into people's heads or read the shape of things to come. I'd never even got that mirror out before Kat came along."

Charlie felt a stab of jealousy. Kat was good at telepathy, Agatha was good at potions, Eliza had been a spellcaster. That just left Charlie. What kind of power did she have? She chewed the edge of her thumb and made a list in her head of all the different types of witches Agatha had mentioned:

Type of witch	Ability	Me
Potions witch	Creates ointments and elixirs	Never made my own. Just followed Agatha's recipes.
Spellcaster	Writes chants	Once used a chant to remove a curse, but didn't write it myself.
Telepathic witch	Can see into another's head	Saw into Kat's head once (ugh, Zak!), but that was down to her talent, not mine.
Elemental witch	Commands wind, water and fire	Hate swimming and am rubbish at lighting fires.
Shape-shifter	Can turn into an animal	Never turned into anything.

"Right," said Agatha, opening her eyes, "while we're out here, Charlie, you might as well practise too."

"Oh, sorry," said Charlie, "my f-file's inside."

Agatha waved her hand. "Don't worry," she said. "You don't need to see everything written down. Now. . ." She reached forward to pick up a small stone, which she placed in front of Charlie. "See if you can move this."

"H-how?"

"With your mind. It's called telekinesis."

"What? I c-can't!"

"Well, you haven't tried yet!" Agatha said. "Concentrate on it – try to tap into the energy that's inside it."

Charlie frowned. It sounded a bit too crazy, even for Agatha. But she sat still and focused on her breathing. Soon she could feel the air around her, hear the trees rustling in the distance, sense the power of the cold earth under her. She tried to focus on the stone. Energy? What was Agatha talking about? She couldn't feel anything coming out of the rock at all.

Just then, there was a cry of surprise from the

cottage. Kat must have seen something in the mirror. A burst of envy rose from deep within Charlie. It passed through her body like a bitter, sharp wind and, just then – just as it tore through her – Charlie sensed the stone. Even with her eyes closed she could see it in front of her; her whole body became aware of its smooth, hard form. She frowned and directed all her jealousy, all her envy, all her rage towards it. A coldness tingled up Charlie's body, running from her toes to the top of her head. It prickled at her nerve-endings, sending a shot of pain and power through her.

Crack!

Charlie opened her eyes. The stone now had a shallow, jagged crevice running through its middle. She *did* have power! Just as much as Kat! She turned to Agatha in delight but the witch's expression was dark.

"Wh-what?" stuttered Charlie.

"Never – *never* – use magic in anger," said Agatha in a stern voice. "What you did just then was dark magic."

"Bu-bu-but it worked!" Charlie didn't understand.

"No!" said Agatha firmly. "Dark magic is *easy*. Any

witch can channel hate and anger and affect things. But in the end that magic is weak. And that's not how we work. That's not how *good* witches work. We use the earth; we connect with nature to help. You didn't *move* the stone, Charlie – you broke it!"

Tears filled Charlie's eyes.

"I . . . I . . . I have to go," she said in a rush. And before Agatha could say another word, Charlie had fled, away from the cottage, through the woods, into her house and up to her bedroom.

Chapter Six
Foul is Fair

Charlie had another dream that night.

She dreamt she heard the familiar chanting from the cellar, like a recording of a poem on repeat. But this time there was something moving in the air above her, buzzing and fizzing as it flew. Charlie held out her hand and a ladybird floated down, down, down and landed in her palm. It was made of stone. It shook itself and shifted its wings, opening one left and the other right. Inside lay a key.

Charlie sat up in bed.

The stone ladybird. It held the key to the trapdoor. Somehow she knew it.

Half-asleep, she stumbled to her desk, reaching

for the ladybird. She shook it and heard the rattle. Charlie put her fingers against the edge of the two wings and pushed. Nothing happened.

She sat down on the floor and closed her eyes. She tried to sense the energy inside it, to feel for the very core of it. Nothing. Charlie sighed in frustration. She was desperate to see Eliza's spell room.

She remembered how she'd cracked the stone earlier that day. She *did* know how to tap into the ladybird's energy, it was just . . . kind of like cheating. Agatha wouldn't like it.

But then, a little voice said inside her, *Agatha wouldn't have to know.*

Maybe she could just use a tiny bit of the power she'd felt earlier. Just once. Just enough to open the ladybird. Then she'd stop and she'd *never* do it again.

Charlie pictured Kat: everyone's favourite. Kat making Agatha laugh, Kat teasing Annie, Kat staring at *Zak*. She felt the icy tingle course through her, the jolt of pain. Then there was a soft *click* and Charlie's eyes flew open. Quickly she put her fingers into the shallow joint and pushed the wings apart. This time they moved. And there was the key, nestled in a hollow in the stone. Charlie lifted it out.

It was small and old, made of a metal that was surprisingly heavy. Charlie's heart quickened – finally, she could see what was in the cellar! Breathless with excitement, she pulled a jumper over her pyjamas, yanked on her trainers, and grabbed a torch.

She pulled the grate of her fireplace aside and, with trembling fingers, fitted the key into the lock. It was stiff, and Charlie had to wiggle it about to find the right spot. *Please work*, she begged. She twisted the key this way and that. Then, all at once, there was a scratching noise, a scraping of metal, and the lock gave way. Charlie pulled the trapdoor open and clicked on the torch. Before her, leading down under the floor, was a set of narrow wooden steps. They curved in a tight spiral, twisting under themselves to darkness below.

Charlie turned backwards to squeeze through the small opening and felt her way, step by step, round and round, under the house to the cellar. She shivered; it was getting colder with every stair. Then her foot struck solid ground; she had reached the bottom.

The moment her foot touched the stone floor, a shiver of electrical current ran up the back of Charlie's spine. The buzz was like thousands of icy needles jabbing into her. Charlie took a fast breath.

She'd never felt anything like it. With a shaking hand she lifted her torch and moved the beam slowly around the room: Eliza's spell room. She swallowed hard, determined to endure the buzzing for as long as she could, as long as it took to investigate.

The room looked a bit like Agatha's cottage, only covered in layers and layers of dust. Cobwebs stretched from the old ceiling beams, twinkling in the light of Charlie's torch – the first light the room had seen for seventeen years.

In the centre was a wooden table covered in bottles and jars of strange ingredients and liquids. There were dried herbs and plants hanging from the ceiling, and crystals dangling from the rafters. But where Agatha's room felt warm and welcoming, Eliza's was cold and foreboding. Feathers were tied in strange shapes and wound around wire, bones were strewn across the table, and a corked jug held some kind of bright red liquid that made Charlie shudder.

She forced her feet to shuffle forward, further into the room. Her ankle brushed against something and, all at once, she felt a rush of warmth: a peace that, for a second, banished the coldness away. Charlie looked down. Touching her ankle was a wood weaving made from honeysuckle twigs – it looked like part of a wreath. Was this one of the blessing wreaths Agatha and Eliza had made together, back before the dark magic took hold? Charlie frowned and looked more closely. The weaving didn't look quite like a wreath – instead of turning in a circle, this one stretched long like a rope. Dried herbs and feathers were intertwined between knots tied in the twigs and there were strange carved markings in the wood.

Charlie moved the torch from side to side around the room and, ahead of her, the light caught the silver shine of lettering. Carefully, Charlie took a step closer. The further she moved away from the wreath, the colder the air felt. On the table in the centre of the room was a large black book: a spell book. It wasn't like Agatha's red one. That one had a gentle feel about it; it made Charlie think of healing and peace. This one was different. It had a jet-black cover, and something was written on the front in curly silver writing – Charlie couldn't quite see the title. She sniffed. The air smelled sour, acidic. She shivered.

Charlie took a nervous step closer. At her footfall, the book seemed to jerk slightly. Was it her imagination or was it tingling? Suddenly she itched to touch it, to open it and see what was inside.

Charlie reached out a shaking finger. The book seemed to arch towards her, the heavy cover bending slightly upwards. Cold wind rushed around her, as if she had just opened the freezer door. A painful buzz of ice shot up through the floor and into her blood. The acidic smell was stronger now, an almost biting scent, acrid in the back of her throat.

Then, with a jolt, Charlie realized. This must be the grimoire Eliza had found! Charlie remembered Agatha talking about it. It was a Book of Shadows: a dark grimoire, full of powerful spells written by a witch hundreds of years ago. Inside the book was the spell Eliza had used to put a curse on Suzy Evans, the curse that had cost Agatha her little finger.

Charlie yanked her hand away in fright. She rushed back round the wooden steps, all the way up into her room, and locked the trapdoor fast behind her. She shoved the little key straight into its hollow and snapped the stone ladybird shut.

There was no way she was going into that room again!

Chapter Seven
If the Broom Fits

Charlie tried hard not to think about the Book of Shadows.

But, for the rest of the week, it was *all* she could think about.

The book filled her mind during the day, and her dreams during the night. It was as if it was calling to her, begging her to come and see it, promising great things if only she would open it. Alone in her bedroom she would hear it somehow. It wasn't *talking*, exactly; it was *moaning*.

Charlie knew what it wanted. To be opened. To be read. To be *used*.

It taunted her, cramming her head with visions

of Zak, everyone's favourite guy. Night after night a sharp, acid scent filled Charlie's room, until it coated the back of her throat with a bitter, sour taste. The smell grew even worse when she thought about Kat. Kat, who was so talented. Kat, who was supposed to be *her* friend, *her* familiar. Kat who was probably hanging out with Zak somewhere.

And then, to her horror, her voice closed up. She tried to tell herself it was just a phase. That she'd be able to speak again soon. But it felt worse than ever. The letters scratched as she tried to pull them out, stinging her chest and scraping her throat, making her feel like she was speaking knives instead of words.

I can help you, moaned the book. *I can soothe your throat. I can bind your friend to you. Only to you.* Charlie tossed and turned in bed, holding her pillow over her ears to block out the noise that was coming from inside her own head.

She struggled through school, sluggishly moving from lesson to lesson, firmly keeping her head down so she wasn't picked on to answer in class. She drifted round the school like a zombie, avoiding eye contact with everyone. She ignored all the gossip in the corridor about Zak Crawford. She ignored all the arguments about who got to carry his bag for him or sit next to him at lunch. She ignored it when a fight broke out between two boys who each wanted to hold the door open for Zak to step through. Even though the school was going mad around her, Charlie kept her head down and walked straight on through the corridors.

And she avoided Kat. Every time she caught sight of bright red hair, Charlie hid, ducking into side corridors or the library.

On Tuesday and Wednesday, Charlie picked up Annie from nursery. She had agreed to look after her, she told herself, and that's why she couldn't go to Agatha's cottage. That was all.

But really she was relieved to have an excuse not to face the witch. How could she tell Agatha what she had done? Her cheeks flushed with shame every time she thought about cracking open the ladybird. She might have some magic talent, but she didn't have much. Not like Agatha and Eliza. Not like Kat.

Wednesday night was the worst of all. She'd spent all afternoon helping Annie with her Halloween costume. They'd found black leggings and a long black top. Charlie had pricked her finger three times sewing a tail on (made out of one leg from a pair of black tights stuffed with newspaper). It had taken her ages – she'd worked until Dad got home. And all Annie had done was complain.

"Don't like it!" She turned her cross face away. "Want red. Red hair like Kat."

"Stop b-being so annoying, Annie!" Charlie snapped at her and Annie burst into tears.

"Hey. . ." Dad came in from the kitchen. He sat down between them on the sofa.

Annie sobbed. "Charlie mean!" She climbed on to Dad's lap and curled her arms around his neck.

Dad took Charlie's hand. "Are you OK, love?" he asked gently. "You haven't been yourself recently."

Charlie tilted her head to rest it on his shoulder. She couldn't tell him anything. Not about the Book of Shadows, not about Zak, not about Kat. In the end she settled for:

"I-I'm just having a t-t-tough time at the moment," she said. Her tight throat made her voice sound croaky.

Annie lifted her head, "Charlie sad?" she asked and she gave Charlie a snotty kiss.

Charlie laughed and wiped it away. "Yes, I'm a bit sad," she admitted. "I'm s-s-sorry I shouted at you, Annie."

Annie climbed from Dad on to Charlie, digging Dad with her elbow as she went.

"You carry on, Annie." Dad puffed in response. "Don't mind me. I didn't need all those ribs anyway."

Annie snuggled into Charlie and Charlie hugged her.

"How are the excavations going?" she asked Dad. "Did you read my book about the wolf?"

"Yes, I did. And you'll be pleased to hear our resident expert thinks they are one and the same! It was a huge beast! No wonder the villagers were scared of it. It took ten arrows to bring it down, apparently."

"Wow!" Charlie could still picture the black-and-white drawing in the book: the power of the wolf's attack, the dark scowling eyes and sharp claws.

"A wolf?" Annie looked from Charlie to Dad.

"Arooo-aroo!" Dad did his best wolf howl. Annie started in fright then burst into giggles.

"Again! Again!"

"Arooo-arooo!" tried Charlie.

"Nah, you sound more like a cockerel," teased Dad.

He sprang to the floor and crouched on all fours, throwing back his head.

"Arooo-arooo!" he howled at the top of his voice.

There was the sound of the front door slamming.

"What on earth is going on here?" Mum said, dropping her work bag on the floor and staring at the three of them.

In the middle of the night Charlie lay awake in the dark, sucking on her finger where she'd pricked it with the needle.

She felt cross with the world. It would be Halloween at the end of next week: Samhain. It was supposed to be such a special night! Charlie had been looking forward to doing the village blessing with Kat. Now it looked like all she'd be doing was taking Annie trick or treating. Well, as long as her three-year-old sister agreed to do all the talking. There was no way Charlie was risking her voice around strangers.

And she could still feel the Book of Shadows

under her floor, begging to be opened. It felt even stronger tonight somehow. Charlie swung her legs out of bed and sat up.

Maybe one peek. Just a little look. She was so tired! Perhaps if she opened it, the book would finally quieten down.

She was just about to pick up the stone ladybird and retrieve the key when she heard a low *Caw*. She opened her curtains. There was a dark shape hovering outside the glass, outlined against the moon. Charlie's eyes took a moment to adjust and then:

"Hopfoot?" she gasped. "W-what are you d-d-doing here?"

She pushed up the wooden sash and the crow fluttered on to her sill.

"Hi," she whispered.

He pushed his head under her hand for her to stroke. Charlie ran her fingers through his feathers. A warmth spread through her cold body. She could resist that book. She had to.

"Th-thanks, Hopfoot," she said. The bird nodded and flew off.

*

On Thursday, Charlie decided enough was enough. She had to face the canteen sometime, even if Kat and Zak were in there together. Squaring her shoulders, she took a tray and chose a sandwich and an apple. She sat down at their usual table and glanced round the room for Kat. There was no sign of her.

Self-consciously, she fiddled with her hair, tucking a curl behind her ears. Just then she noticed Zak – being waved to the front of the lunch queue, of course. A Year 7 boy with freckles was carrying his tray for him while Zak pointed to things he wanted. Charlie rolled her eyes and watched every head turn to look at him as he walked past. To her astonishment, he stopped in front of her table.

Charlie clenched her teeth as she watched Freckles practically bowing to Zak.

"Hi, Banana," said Zak with a grin, casually sitting down next to her.

Charlie groaned inwardly – she was dreading having to speak. Her throat felt scratchy so she quickly poured herself a bit of water and took a mouthful without thinking.

Ew! For a moment she'd forgotten that the school

water tasted like vinegar. She swallowed the sharp liquid fast and looked back at Zak.

The sun was hitting his hair from the side, making the deep brown a kind of chocolate colour. He smiled, his eyes warm and friendly.

Charlie felt a sudden wave of guilt. He'd had a tough time at his old school and here was Charlie, always being mean to him. She knew herself what it was like starting a new school. She should have been nicer, more welcoming. She smiled back. He wasn't that bad! He was just teasing her. Almost of its own accord, her body leaned forward and her hand met the fabric of his jumper—

A jolt of electricity flew through her body.

Magic. There was magic. She could feel it tingling, but it was a cold tingling, like when Charlie had broken that stone – like in Eliza's spell room. She caught a very faint acidic smell . . . and her mind made a sudden leap:

Zak is a witch!

Charlie's hand froze. She snatched it back in shock. Zak looked up at her, recognition in his eyes.

"I ha-have to g-go," she managed to stammer out. She grabbed her bag, abandoning her sandwich in her rush to squeeze past Zak. She fled down the corridor, her heart thumping wildly. Her eyes searched for somewhere to hide, somewhere Zak wouldn't go. *The girls' toilet*. She pushed open the door and flung herself into a cubicle.

There she sat, staring at the inside of the cubicle door, her thoughts going round like an earworm: *Zak is a witch! Zak is a witch!*

Could that be true?

School *had* felt odd in the last few weeks – there was a tension in the air, like the *ting* of a high-pitched tuning fork in the background. Charlie had thought it was just her – that the strain was due to her loneliness, her fight to resist the Book of Shadows. But, now she thought about it, those weren't the only factors. Everyone had been arguing a lot more recently. Arguing about Zak. As Zak fever had spread across the school, that boy had become practically the only topic of conversation.

Had he done something to cause the obsession? Something magic?

She cast her mind back to Zak's first day at school. He'd been so arrogant – rude to everyone. Almost like he didn't need to try. . .

"I don't think I'll need help making friends," he'd said.

Charlie dropped her head in her hands. So many things were falling into place.

Then, in the canteen, she herself had had a sudden desire to be friends with him. Why? Could he have. . . Had he done something to her? She made her way through the corridor for science class, her mind filled with thoughts flitting around like butterflies.

Science that day was all about the total lunar eclipse. The eclipse was due in ten days' time, on the thirty-first. It should have been a really interesting lesson, but Charlie could barely concentrate. All she could think about was Zak. While she was supposed to be drawing a diagram of the sun, earth and moon, Charlie made a list of all the ways Zak could be using magic to make people like him:

Hypnotism? How? No pocket watch or snake. Through his eyes??
Some kind of persuasion spell? Mind-control thingy?

Voodoo doll? – but he can't make dolls of everyone in the school!
Some kind of gas? Or magic candle? – maybe he's lit one somewhere? But wouldn't that set off the smoke alarm?

(Charlie knew all too well what happened when you lit a candle in school.)

Enchanted food? Drink?

Drink. She gave a quick gasp.

"Charlotte?" Mr Fisher looked up at the noise. "Are you all right?"

Charlie turned bright red and nodded frantically at her teacher. She blushed and pretended to colour in the moon. When Mr Fisher had gone back to his marking, Charlie took out her notepad again and wrote:

Something in the water?

Chapter Eight

Take a Sip from My Secret Potion

When the bell rang, Charlie rushed out of school. She had to see Agatha and Kat. Now. She didn't care what had happened that week – she needed to tell them her news. Charlie ran through the woods and into Agatha's cottage at full pelt.

"Whoa!" called Agatha. She and Kat were sitting at the table sipping tea. "What's happened?"

"Z-Z-Z-Zak," Charlie burst out, breathless, "He's a w-w-w-witch!"

There was a moment of silence, and then:

"What are you talking about?" said Kat. Her tone was defensive.

"I felt it . . ." Charlie ignored Kat and looked at

Agatha "... when I touched him. A b-buzzing. It was cold magic ... like s-s-something wrong. And there's more." She paused and took in a deep breath. "He's done something to everyone in the school... I know it. It's some k-k-k-kind of sp-sp-sp..." Her throat closed in. "... charm," she managed. "I think he's done it by putting something in the water."

"That doesn't make sense." Kat's voice was scornful and dismissive.

"I-I-I'm the only p-person who hasn't been dr-drinking it, but today I drank s-s-s-some and, after I did, I l-l-liked him." Charlie was tripping over her words to explain. It was all so clear in her head, but she couldn't tell the story fast enough.

"You liked him because he's nice," said Kat.

"No. It's m-m-magic," said Charlie.

"It's not, Charlie!" Kat was shouting now. "You're being ridiculous! He's just a nice person. Come to lunch with us and you'll see!"

"Us?"

"Yeah – we've been having lunch together sometimes."

"I kn-kn-knew it!" All Charlie's rage came boiling to the surface.

"Well at least I've got more than one friend!" Kat glared at Charlie pointedly.

"He's not your fr-fr-friend! I told you!" Charlie was nearly choking to get the words out. "He p-p-put something in the water!"

"I'm not listening to any more of this!" Kat yelled. She turned on her heel and marched out. Hopfoot took off from the window sill and flew after her.

Charlie burst into tears.

"I know it's t-t-true," she sobbed. "I know that's wh-what he did." She scowled through her tears. "But you p-p-p-probably won't believe me either."

Agatha looked at Charlie thoughtfully for a moment, and then said, "I do believe you."

"Really?" Charlie said doubtfully.

Agatha gave a short nod. "Yes. But we need to be sure," she said. "Can you get some of that water and bring it here? Then we'll see if you are right."

"I'll g-get it tomorrow."

"Good." Agatha put her hands together. There was something imploring about her gaze. "We must resolve this. You need your familiar," she said simply.

Charlie looked down. It was true. Kat was far

stronger than her, much better at magic. Without Kat she was useless.

That night, Charlie barely slept.

The row with Kat ate away at her, gnawing at her bones every time she began to nod off. It felt like everything good was broken. They'd had such a bond, she and Kat; and now, one boy, one magic spell had come between them.

Maybe, moaned the Book of Shadows silently, *maybe Kat was never really your familiar.*

Charlie turned over in bed.

Maybe she was just with you when she thought you were the only witch in town. Now she has Zak to learn magic with instead.

Cold nausea flooded Charlie. She could hear the Book of Shadows taunting her from the cellar, and she gripped the sheets to stop herself going through the fireplace to find it.

On Friday morning there was no Kat at the meeting place, no Kat at break, and no Kat at lunch. A whole week had now gone by since they'd last hung out at school together. And Charlie had never felt so alone.

It wasn't as easy as she expected to get a sample of water. In the canteen there were jugs on every table, but the moment a full jug was placed down, it was snatched up, and every last drop was carefully and fairly measured out around the table to make sure each person got the same amount. Charlie looked at the sea of faces. This was where it didn't help that she had no friends! Then she spotted the girl she'd helped the other day. The girl with the yellow hairclips. Charlie took a deep breath. She got her words ready, rubbing the tip of her tongue against the roof of her mouth to unlock it. *Please don't stammer*, she begged her body. *Please.*

She walked over to Hairclips, who was rationing out the canteen jug.

"H-hi," said Charlie.

Hairclips looked up. She frowned for a moment, then remembered. "Oh, hi!" she said brightly.

"C-c-could I have a bit of water?" Charlie asked.

"Okaaay," Hairclips answered, reluctantly. "But just a bit. Only up to the first line." Carefully, she poured the liquid into Charlie's water bottle. She held it up so everyone could check Charlie hadn't been given more than her fair share.

"There," said Hairclips.

"Thanks," mumbled Charlie, and she rushed out of the canteen, the bottle in her hands.

The bottle sat in her bag for the rest of the school day. Charlie could hardly concentrate on her lesson. The thought of the liquid filled her head. There was something about it that was highly addictive. Even though Charlie hated its sharp flavour, she had to try really hard to stop herself reaching into her bag and taking a sip. Now that she had tasted it once, she longed for the cool fresh liquid. She pictured it slipping down the back of her throat, filling her tummy. All around her other students had their own bottles out on the desks and were swigging from them merrily.

Charlie impatiently watched the minutes tick by. She couldn't seem to concentrate, couldn't make her mind slow down. It bounced from the water, to Zak, to Kat and, all the while, visions of the Book of Shadows hovered at the edges of her thoughts.

When the last bell rang, Charlie set off through the woods to Agatha's cottage. At last, she might be able to find some answers.

*

"I got some," Charlie cried, bursting through the door and shaking her bottle triumphantly. She looked round the room and gave silent thanks that Kat wasn't there. She couldn't bear another row. "Wh-wh-what now?"

"Now we try to make the spell reveal its magic," said Agatha in a matter-of-fact voice. She reached up to a high shelf and took down a small leather drawstring purse. She tipped the contents out on to her palm and Charlie gazed down to see five coloured stones. Agatha selected a blue one:

"*Lapis lazuli*," she said. "The truth stone."

She poured the water into a little pan and put it on the heat. Soon it bubbled and spat. Steam began to rise.

Charlie felt a moment of doubt. What if, after all that, there was nothing wrong with the water? Maybe Kat was right and Charlie *was* just jealous. If so, she'd argued with her best friend for nothing. And, worst of all, it would mean Kat had chosen Zak of her own free will.

Agatha took the stone and then, to Charlie's astonishment, raised it to her eye. She looked for a long moment and then handed the gemstone to Charlie.

"What do you see?" she asked. "Look at the steam through the stone and tell me."

Puzzled, Charlie copied Agatha, lifting the stone to her eye-level. It was solid blue and at first she couldn't see anything through it at all. But as she focused, her eyes found a thin vein of white inside the blue. The more she stared at it, the more transparent it became and soon, to her surprise, she found she could see past it, as if she was looking through the crack under a door. There was the fire and the pan and the steam. She peered into the billowing mist. It swirled and danced in front of her; then, all at once, it turned a bright green. Tiny sparks of ice jumped in the steam. They looked like little hands joining together. Charlie cried out.

"That's dark magic," said Agatha quietly. "Do you see the hands, the way they are linked together? That's some kind of possession spell."

Charlie put down the stone and looked into Agatha's eyes.

"You were right, Charlie," the witch said.

Charlie let out a breath she hadn't even realized she was holding. *She was right.* Kat had been tricked, along with everyone else at school. Her throat opened. The bitter taste lifted and somehow the words inside her felt less sharp, less scratchy.

"What does it do exactly, that spell?" Charlie spoke without her stutter for the first time in ages.

"It draws people to you, attracts them."

Suddenly, Charlie remembered what Dad had said in the car about Zak having had a rough time at his old school. "I think he w-wanted to be liked," she said. "Maybe he thought this was the only way."

Agatha sighed and shook her head.

"What kind of sp-spell is it? How is he putting it into the water?"

"I don't know," Agatha admitted. "But we need to find out fast. The more Zak controls people's minds, the more he risks hurting them permanently. Every day that those children drink the charmed water they are falling deeper under the spell. It's addictive. The spell will build and build and soon Zak will be all they think about."

"How can I f-find out?"

"Well, you could try the simplest method."

"What's that?"

"Ask him."

Chapter Nine

We Found a Witch!

Through the night Charlie puzzled through whether she should tell Kat what they'd found out – that there was proof that Zak was a witch. On a bit of paper she scribbled the pros and cons:

Pros	Cons
K would know I'm right.	Might sound a bit showy-offy. K still might not believe me.
K might be my friend again.	Only might.
Don't want to exclude her.	Haven't found out exactly how he did it yet. . .

In the end, this final "con" point rang out for Charlie. She would confront Zak, find out more, and then Kat would have to believe her. At midnight, Charlie finally rolled over and fell asleep.

In the morning Charlie woke up with a plan.

"Dad?" she said as she sat down at the breakfast table. She kept her voice light. "Are you g-g-going up to Broom Hill today?"

"Yep." He was zipping up a large bag of tools.

"Can I c-come?"

"Sure." He sounded surprised but pleased. "Have breakfast, then we'll go."

Mum had made pancakes. Annie had insisted on spreading the chocolate on hers all by herself and there was now more chocolate on her face than on her pancake.

Charlie kissed her chocolaty forehead affectionately. "Any l-left for me?"

"Just about," said Mum. "Matt had a pile of them earlier."

"Matt? What's he d-doing up before noon on a Saturday?"

"He's gone to rehearsal again."

Ah. Charlie had heard the sounds from his room last night:

"Bubble bubble toil and trouble," and then a *lot* of cackling.

"What are you d-doing today, Mum?"

"Annie and I are sorting out the rest of the loft, aren't we, Annie?"

Annie nodded and smeared more chocolate on herself.

"There's still lots to organize up there," Mum continued. "Loads of Bess's old stuff." She tweaked the green silk scarf round her neck. "I might find some other bits and pieces to wear!"

"Want?" Annie held out a half-chewed pancake.

"Umm ... thanks..." Charlie took the soggy mess. "Mmm!" she pretended to eat it behind her hand.

Annie clapped.

In the car, Charlie's mind was whirring. She hoped her instincts were right – that Zak would turn up at the hill sometime today. There was something about the place that fascinated her and every bone in her body was telling her Zak felt the same pull.

"I'll be over there again, in that tent." Dad pointed as he held out a helmet and jacket for Charlie. "Come and get me when you want to go home."

Charlie headed towards the pit she'd seen before. The big deep triangle was empty now. All the artefacts had been removed and given to the museum, but still the earth buzzed with a cold dark magic. Charlie stared down into the soil below.

"I knew you'd come, Banana," said a voice at her side.

Charlie turned her head.

It was the first time she'd seen Zak since she'd worked out what he was. He stood beside her, his arms crossed and his head high. He looked directly at Charlie, as if challenging her to begin. For a second she wasn't sure what to say, but then she remembered Agatha's advice: keep it simple.

"You're a witch," she said bluntly.

There was a moment of silence. Charlie could see Zak hesitating. Then he grinned widely.

"Yes," he said with a note of pride in his voice. "At least, I think I am. I've always been able to do weird stuff, you know?" he shrugged. "You're one too." He tilted his head. "I can tell."

Charlie nodded in answer.

"It's Kat I can't work out." He dimpled the side of his mouth. "She's magic, but . . . she's different somehow."

"She's my, my f-familiar," said Charlie. "We do magic together – I'm much stronger with her."

Zak frowned at that, puzzled.

Charlie leaned towards him.

"What did you d-do, Zak? To the w-water I mean."

He gave a laugh. "I just gave myself a bit of help!"

Charlie raised her eyebrows. Zak sighed.

"At my last school, everyone thought I was weird," he explained. "They used to call me Wacky Zak. They said I was crazy. I felt like I didn't fit in anywhere."

Charlie watched him closely. As cross as she was with him, she did know what he meant. Before Charlie had understood her power she'd felt like the odd one out too.

"No one liked me. Not one person." His voice cracked. "There was no way I was risking *that* happening at my new school."

Charlie waited.

"It was just one chant," he said. "Quite easy, actually. Bit of powder on a tap, a few words, some top-notch witch skills, and *poof*! Everyone likes me!"

"So you're t-t-tricking people into liking you."

Zak shrugged. "Those kids don't know any different! I'm not *harming* them!"

"You're con-controlling their minds! It's dark magic!"

"You're making it sound so evil. It's just one spell."

"How did you know how to do it?"

"I found it in a book – there. . ." He jerked a thumb down into the pit, where they'd found the apothecary remains. "I knew it was magic straight away. It felt weird: fizzy, you know?" He looked at Charlie and a cold finger of fear ran down her spine. "I managed to slip it into my rucksack when no one was looking."

"What k-kind of book?" Charlie asked the question, but she already knew the answer. There was only one type of book that would contain a possession spell: a book of dark magic. A Book of Shadows.

"Why?" Zak looked suspicious. "You can't see it. It's mine. I found it and I'm not giving you the spells in it, if that's what you're hoping." He was getting agitated.

"Zak – c-calm down. I don't w-want your book."

Zak relaxed his shoulders at that. His eyes were bright. "It's so cool!" He shook his head in awe. "Before I could only do little things. Bits and pieces of magic. But now. . ." He grinned. "I've got so many amazing recipes at my fingertips! The book keeps suggesting more spells. It's like we're working *together*. With the book I'm going to be so powerful – I know it!"

As Zak spoke the sharp buzzing around him became stronger and stronger, like a harsh itching in Charlie's bones.

"Zak – that grim-grim. . ." She swapped the word. "That *book* is full of dark magic. It's dangerous."

"What do *you* know?" Zak said dismissively. He kicked a loose bit of soil and it tumbled into the pit before them.

"I know it c-c-calls to you," said Charlie softly.

Zak's eyes narrowed in suspicion.

"I found a b-b-book of dark magic too," Charlie confessed. "But I won't use it."

"Scared, are you, Banana?"

Charlie ignored that. She didn't want to admit to the nights she'd spent shaking with fright at the thought of the book, of the thought of giving in to it. "You have to stop," was all she said.

Zak leaned in close to her. "Well, why don't you make me?" he dared her. "Open up your book and find something to stop me. You know you want to."

Charlie made her hands into fists. He was right. Ever since she'd found the Book of Shadows she'd been itching to use it. She'd had to hold herself back from running to the cellar and opening it.

"No!" she said firmly. "I won't t-t-touch dark m-m-magic, and you shouldn't either."

"Like I said," Zak said as he crossed his arms, "stop me if you can, Charlie." He looked right at her and Charlie shivered in response.

Zak laughed again, and then started walking away. "See ya!" he called over his shoulder, whistling as he went.

Charlie burst into Agatha's cottage.

"He's g-g-got a book of dark magic! A Book of Shadows!"

Agatha turned pale. Charlie slumped into the armchair and tried to catch her breath.

"He says he found it on B-Broom Hill. He used a spell in it to make a powder!"

The old witch breathed in sharply. After a moment she spoke. "I know that book," she said. "At least, I know *of* it."

Charlie sat up straighter to listen.

"In the olden days all kinds of witches lived up on the hill," said Agatha. "Each house was a sort of mini-coven. Most of the covens used white magic: healing potions, weather spells, chants to help crops grow – that type of thing. But there was one coven that was different: a pair of witches who used magic for darker purposes."

Charlie leaned forward in the chair.

"That coven was known as the Snake Sisters. The two witches dealt in curses, hexes and jinxes. Villagers came to them for revenge spells; for potions to trick someone; for chants to harm a rival's crops, or to give acne to an enemy. The sisters each had a powerful Book of Shadows, full of dark spells.

"One of them perished at the hands of the witch hunter in the 1600s. The other sister escaped. She fled to the woods to hide and no one knew what happened to her.

"In our day, hundreds of years after the Snake Sisters, Eliza found the escaped witch's diary and her Book of Shadows in the woods. She became obsessed with her and with the book." Agatha took a deep breath. "Zak must have found the other grimoire at Broom Hill. It must have been hidden for all these years, until the archaeological dig brought it to light."

Charlie froze. Eliza's grimoire – the one she had found in the spell room – had once belonged to the Snake Sisters! She opened her mouth to say something, but Agatha was still talking.

"I don't know what spell Zak used," Agatha said as she flipped through her own grimoire, "I don't have any dark magic spells in here and, without knowing what he did to the water, it's hard to take the spell off." Agatha shut her book in frustration. The soft red cover slammed closed, releasing a warm, spicy scent into the cottage.

"Are the d-d-dark magic spells all the same in every Book of Shadows?" Charlie asked.

"They can differ, but broadly, yes. Spells are

handed down across the generations and they usually contain more or less the same ingredients. It's a bit like a recipe book. Why?"

"Because, because. . ." Charlie took a deep breath. She knew she had to say it. . . "Because I can get a book of d-dark magic!"

"What do you mean?" said Agatha quickly.

Charlie bit her lip. Suddenly she wasn't sure why she'd kept the secret of Eliza's room for so long. All in a rush the story came tumbling out: how she'd found the cellar window, and how she knew there must be a room down there; how she'd heard the key rattling inside the stone ladybird. Here she paused. She could feel her face growing warm as she skipped over *exactly* how she'd got the key out. Finally she told Agatha about Eliza's spell room.

"It was horrible! C-cold and sour. I h-hated it in there. And the book was the worst of all!" Charlie shivered. "The air around it was s-s-s-so sharp and icy."

Agatha sat down on the rug all in a heap. She stared into the fire for a long time. Charlie didn't dare interrupt her thoughts. When the witch eventually spoke it was in a low, strained voice.

"I remember that spell room. Eliza loved it down there. The entrance used to be in your kitchen. We would spend the day together mixing potions and writing spells. At night, by the fire in the Akelarre, the few remaining witches would come over and we'd all swap stories and recipes. That was before everything changed."

Agatha's knuckles were white as she clenched her hands together.

"The Snake Sister's diary Eliza found in the woods – it described the witch's escape from the hill and the trial of her sister." Agatha shook her head. "What the Witchfinder General did to those poor women was horrible. He hurt so many, even the ones who used white magic. Eliza wouldn't let herself forget. She wanted to honour the old witches, the ones who had died. She threw herself into darker and darker magic, trying to connect with witches from the past, trying to summon them. She grew more and more worried about being discovered. She enchanted the cellar window so it wouldn't open and sealed over the kitchen entrance with magic. I never knew how she got in and out of the cellar herself – she kept it a secret."

Agatha's dark eyes grew purple.

"Charlie, have you touched that book?" she asked.

Charlie squirmed. "No. But it . . . it's calling to me," she confessed. "I can hear it, in the night."

Agatha nodded. "You did well to resist," she said. She stood up abruptly. "But we need it now if we're to reveal the spell behind the possession." She reached into a drawer in her table and pulled out a piece of fabric. It was pure white, soft and shimmering in the firelight.

"Mulberry silk," said Agatha. Gently she folded the silk over and over and put it into a fabric bag for Charlie. "Wrap the book in this. It's the only way to touch it safely. Then bring it straight here."

"W-what?" Charlie asked. "You mean g-g-g-go into the cellar and get it?"

"Yes. Tonight."

Charlie swallowed hard, trying to push away the feeling of dread.

"You can do it." Agatha sat down firmly. "The fact that you haven't touched the book, that you haven't used dark magic since you broke the stone. . ."

"Um. . ." Charlie began, interrupting her.

Agatha stopped. She looked at her from the

armchair, straight and still. Her gloved hands were folded neatly in her lap. Charlie suddenly felt like she'd been sent to see the head.

"I—" she began and stopped again. She took a deep breath; "I used d-d-dark magic," she confessed. Tears filled her eyes. "I w-w-wanted to open the ladybird t-to see Eliza's room. I'm sorry!" A trickle ran down her cheeks.

Agatha stood. She came over to Charlie and took hold of her hands.

"Charlie, you did so well," she said.

Charlie frowned in confusion.

"Not many witches could have resisted that book," Agatha continued. "Dark magic is strong. It calls to witches, tempting them down the wrong path, taking over their thoughts until there's almost nothing left. But you resisted it. Night after night you refused to give in."

Agatha smoothed Charlie's curls. "You don't need dark magic." She gave Charlie a flash of a smile. "You're going to be a powerful witch without it."

"I am? But. . ." Suddenly she was desperate to come clean. "I don't have a special t-t-t-talent!"

"No," Agatha said slowly, and Charlie's heart

sank. The witch drew back and studied her. "You don't have *one* talent," she continued.

"What do you m-m-mean?"

"You are what is known as an *eclectic* witch."

Charlie blinked.

"That means you have a talent for lots of different types of magic. As time goes on you will learn to control your powers, and then you can take a bit from each branch – a bit of elemental magic and potions magic and telepathy, and so on – and use them as you need them."

"Is th-that good?"

Agatha laughed. "Yes. It's very good indeed!" she said. "You are going to be very strong. That's why I'm so hard on you. That's why you mustn't use dark magic. Dark magic feels easy and it's very tempting to use it, but, once you go down that route, it will lead you further and further away from goodness. Promise me you'll never use it, not even once more."

Charlie breathed out slowly.

"I swear I never will," she said. And she meant it.

Chapter Ten
Wicked

In her bedroom, Charlie waited until the household had gone to sleep.

She sat herself down on the floor, and then closed her eyes. She tried to sense the ladybird, to feel it unlocking.

Nope.

Again and again she tried, until she was ready to scream in frustration.

She took a breath. She thought back to what Agatha had said. She was a strong witch – an *eclectic* witch. She could do this.

She focused in on the ladybird again, looking for its centre, its essence. She was met with cold hard stone. It was no use.

Without dark magic it was hard!

Charlie leaned back against the wall in despair.

Her head was pounding, as if something was knocking on the inside of her brain, pushing to get out. She could hear the Book of Shadows calling to her, feel the tingle of dark magic rising through her body against her will.

"No," she whispered, her voice weak as she tried to cast the sensation aside. Her empty hands moved helplessly before her, grasping nothing but air. The book. The book would help her. All she had to do was use a tiny bit of dark magic, unlock the ladybird, step into the cellar and open the black leather cover. Inside there would be a spell to stop Zak.

"*Stop me if you can, Charlie.*" Zak's taunt floated into her head.

Come and find me, Charlie, moaned the Book of Shadows silently. *I'll stop Zak.*

Charlie's legs twitched. An aching spread across the backs of her calves. She stretched her legs out and they wiggled her body towards the grate. It was almost as though she was being dragged towards the secret entrance.

"No," she whispered again. She was terrified that,

once down there, she wouldn't find the strength to wrap up the book. Instead she would open it greedily and devour whatever was inside.

"Help," she croaked into the darkness. "Help me."

A vision fluttered into her mind, pale and shaky. "Hold on!" it said. "I'm coming!"

It was... It was Kat! Kat – transparent and wobbly inside her head.

"I'm coming!" said the vision again and Charlie put her dizzy head in her hands, scrunching up her body like a hedgehog, holding her limbs tight to stop herself reaching for the book below.

She lay there for what felt like hours. Then she heard a noise, a soft rattle on her window. Scarcely daring to hope, she pulled herself wearily across the room and opened her curtains. In the moonlight below she saw a small figure, holding a pebble, ready to throw. Charlie stared in amazement. She opened the window and called down.

"K-Kat? Is that r-r-really you?" Suddenly the strength came flooding back through Charlie's body. "I'm c-coming down," she whispered and she tiptoed down the stairs to the front door and unlocked it as quickly as she could.

She practically fell into Kat's arms.

"I saw you!" Kat was whispering. "I saw you in my head!"

Charlie was light-headed with relief. Kat! She'd come! "I-I'm sorry," Charlie began, but Kat stopped her.

"No, *I'm* sorry, Charlie," she said. "I'm so sorry I didn't believe you. I don't know what I was thinking. All week I couldn't stop wanting to be with Zak. But when I saw you in my head just now, something switched inside me. It was as though I'd just woken up. Of course I believe you! You're my witch, my best friend. If you think something funny is going on, then I'm with you."

"Really?" Charlie asked shyly. "You really mean that?"

"Of course." Kat nodded so firmly her huge glasses slipped down her nose. She grinned and pushed them up again. Charlie felt a sudden rush of love for her friend. It warmed her from her scalp to her toes. She grinned back at the familiar. They were a team again.

"Now," said Kat, back to business. "Let's go and test the water—"

"It's OK," Charlie broke in. "Agatha and I have already done it. I took some to her cottage in a bottle and she tested it."

"And?"

"It's a spell. A p-possession spell."

"Ohhh," Kat moaned. "You were right. I'm sorry! I'm sorry!" she repeated.

"It doesn't matter," said Charlie, smiling. And it really didn't. "You're here now! Come inside and I'll fill you in!"

Kat stared open-mouthed as Charlie finished the tale. They were sitting on Charlie's bed, whispering as the house around them slept.

"There's *really* a book of dark magic in this house?" she said finally.

"In the cellar."

"Then let's go get it," said Kat. "Before it does you any more damage."

"But I can't open this." Charlie gestured at the stone ladybird. "And without the key we can't get in. . ."

"Of course you can open it," Kat said encouragingly. "We'll do it together."

Kat shuffled over and sat in front of Charlie. She took Charlie's hands in her own and Charlie felt a warm hum run through her palms. Kat closed her eyes and Charlie did the same. They had sat this way so many times before, performing magic, and Charlie just hoped that together they would be strong enough for this.

She focused in on the ladybird, pushing the tempting cold buzzing away and filling her mind with warm thoughts. She felt a rush of energy from the familiar opposite her, flooding her body with heat. This time there was no pain, no sharpness. Instead, she was bathed in a soft glow. She smiled, feeling the magic course through her.

Click!

She couldn't believe it. The lock of the ladybird had sprung open.

As quickly as she could, Charlie pulled the wings aside. She showed Kat the tiny key.

Kat couldn't keep still. She jumped up and bounced from foot to foot, her green eyes flashing.

"Come on, come on!" she said, darting over to the fireplace.

Charlie's hands shook as she fit the key in the

lock. She couldn't help remembering how it felt down there: so dark and dank and heavy with sadness. She fiddled with the key until they heard a low *pop*. Charlie pulled the trapdoor up.

"Wow!" Kat breathed, pointing her torch into the blackness below. "I can't believe you went down there on your own!" She took off a pretend hat to Charlie and bowed. "You are one brave witch!"

Charlie felt a glow of pride. She turned round into the gap and felt for each narrow step with her foot. Kat followed. Down, down they climbed, twisting as they followed the spiral steps.

At the bottom Charlie swung her torch around the spell room and shivered.

"Ew. It's creepy down here," Kat whispered, staring at the bones and feathers.

"I know." Charlie shivered, trying to shake off the cold buzzing in the air. Now she was closer she could hear the book louder than ever, pulling her towards it, tempting her to open it. Charlie clenched her teeth and shook her head.

"What is it?" Kat asked in concern.

"The b-b-book." She pointed with her head.

Kat gasped. "It's glowing!" she cried. "But it's

weird. It's not a warm, soft glow, like you and Agatha have; it has a kind of cold green light."

Charlie clenched her hands to stop herself reaching out and touching it. Instead she pulled out the folded silk and shook it open. Inside her head she heard a low moan. In a flash she knew: the book hated the silk. She could feel it shrink back, begging her not to wrap it up. She tried to step forward but her feet refused to move. Her arms trembled and the silk fluttered in her hands like a sail.

"I can't d-d-do it!" Charlie cried out.

Kat swallowed hard. "It's awful down here," she said, nearly in tears. "It's hurting my eyes!"

Suddenly Charlie felt like she was suffocating, like the coldness was filling her from her toes to her mouth, drowning her in sharp iciness. "We need to get out!" she cried, stepping back.

"What's this?" Kat touched her arm, gently stopping her escape. The familiar was staring down at the long wreath Charlie had seen last time. "This . . . this bit of weaving – the air is different around here. It's warmer somehow. . ." Kat sat on the dusty floor, next to the long honeysuckle plait.

Her hand reached out and touched the plait,

running her fingers over every bump in the wood. Charlie watched as Kat closed her eyes.

"That feels better," she said.

Charlie gasped as a rush of heat from Kat hit her, filling her body with strength. For a moment the cold and pain rushed away, flowing out through her toes. As fast as she could, before the warmth disappeared, Charlie darted forward towards the table. She steeled herself and lifted the pure silk. She ignored the moans of the book and threw the silk over it, wrapping the fabric around and around the Book of Shadows until it was silent.

Together the friends ran out of the spell room, stumbling up the stairs and bursting into Charlie's room in relief. Charlie slammed the trapdoor hard behind them. With shaking hands, she shoved the bound book into her bag.

"Is it still calling you?" Kat asked.

"No," said Charlie breathlessly. "That silk is h-holding it. I wouldn't like to unwrap it though!"

"Thank goodness for that wreath," said Kat. "Whatever it is, it's the only bit of white magic left in that spell room."

Then she looked at Charlie. "I can't believe you

had to go in there alone," she said. "I'm sorry." She put her head in her hands. "I'm so, so sorry."

"N-n-not this again! It's OK. R-really!"

"I didn't listen to you. And I didn't notice anything was odd about Zak. I'm such a rubbish familiar."

"Don't be r-ridiculous!"

"I can't seem to do anything right!" Kat sniffed. "How did I not notice that something was up?"

"You were under a spell!"

"And I didn't even realize! You did – you knew the water was enchanted just from the smell of it." Kat's voice rose in frustration. "And I can't make the scrying mirror work – I've tried for hours!"

Charlie looked at her in surprise. "But I thought you m-m-managed to do it the other d-day?"

"Nah. I can't see anything in that black glass. All I managed to do was knock it over. Honestly. . ." She fiddled with her glasses. "I don't think I've got any talent at all!" She gave a forced laugh, then her eyes welled up. "I don't think I'm of any help to you." A little sob escaped her.

"Oh, Kat!" Charlie moved closer and put her arm around her friend. "You're my b-best friend." She squeezed Kat's shoulder. "We're a pair. Anyway. I should be saying sorry too." Charlie took a deep breath. "I was so jealous," she admitted.

"You didn't need to be!" Kat cried. "I missed you!"

"B-but you were too busy hanging out with Z-Z-Zak?"

"We only had lunch twice," said Kat. "The other days I had lunchtime detention." She stretched out her legs on the floorboards and sighed. "I really don't know why the school can't get used to my tights," she said, wiggling her stripy legs.

Chapter Eleven

A Charm of Powerful Trouble

"We got it!" Charlie carefully put the book, swaddled in cloth, on Agatha's table. "I n-nearly couldn't do it, but then . . . Kat c-came and helped me."

Agatha looked at Kat, who nodded.

"I had a vision of Charlie last night," the familiar said. "She was in need of my help. Somehow that set me free from Zak's spell – all I could think about was getting to Charlie. I can't believe I was so stupid."

Agatha shook her head. "You were under a very powerful spell," she said gently. Then she looked at the Book of Shadows. "It's strong." She breathed in. On the table, a fat candle flickered. "Poor Eliza."

Agatha's voice was so quiet it was as though she was talking to herself. "Once the book had her in its grasp, she was lost." She stroked the silk. "My poor friend."

Charlie and Kat waited, neither wanting to interrupt.

Agatha let out a breath. "Right," she said in her brisk voice. "I know it's the middle of the night but there's no time to lose. We need to find out what spell Zak used."

Charlie drew back. She was terrified of unwrapping the book.

"It's OK," said Agatha. "We're going to neutralize it first."

Charlie frowned.

"We're going to put the book into a kind of trance, so we can look inside. Like an anaesthetic."

"Okaaay," said Charlie, hesitantly.

"What kind of herbs would we need, Charlie?"

"Um. . ." Charlie tried to remember all her lessons. She reached for her file, where the herbs were neatly listed in rows. Agatha stopped her with her hand.

"No," she said softly. "Close your eyes and feel your way."

Charlie shut her eyes. She pictured the cold harsh

buzzing. What would stop it? An image filled her mind: a soft meadow of grass. . .

"Dandelion," she said. "And something gentle . . . mint . . . and . . . and cinnamon for warmth." When she opened her eyes Agatha was pounding the three ingredients in a pestle and mortar.

"Did . . . did I g-g-get it right?" she asked.

"You're the one who's been in that spell room, Charlie. You're the one who felt the book calling."

Charlie nodded. It was right. She felt it.

"Now you need to write a spell." Agatha looked at Charlie.

"Me?"

"Yes."

"But I . . . I've never done that b-before. I don't know what to s-s-s-say!"

"Calm down," said Agatha as she sprinkled the powder on the silk. "Just say what comes naturally."

Charlie shook her head in doubt. Then she felt Kat's warm hand on her arm. All at once Charlie was filled with energy and light. Without pausing for thought, she plunged on, letting her body feel the way. To her surprise, she felt the tingle of magic and, when her mouth opened she spoke in a clear loud voice:

"Sleep, sleep,
In warmth and peace.
Sleep, sleep,
Relax, release."

There was a soft sigh from under the wrapping.

"You did it!" Kat squeezed Charlie's arm. "Your first spell!"

Charlie grinned. She'd no idea *how* she'd done it; it had just poured out of her somehow. One thing she did know. "I did it with your help," she told her familiar.

Carefully Agatha unwrapped the book. It was quiet now; Charlie couldn't feel it buzzing. She leaned forward to see. The cover was old, made of rough cracked leather. In silver writing were the words:

THE BOOK OF SHADOWS

The B and the S were highly decorated with swirls and sigils, and tiny stars surrounded the letters. Inside, silver writing spread across jet-black pages like a wandering spider.

Agatha flicked through the recipes, shaking her head at the more unpleasant ones, until. . .

"Here." She pointed to a page.

POSSESSION: A SPELL TO CHARM THE MINDS OF THOSE AROUND YOU.

COPPER POWDER

WHITE VINEGAR

RUE

WATER

"This is it!" cried Charlie. She could still taste the vinegar at the back of her throat. She read on. There was a chant listed below:

BY THE DARKNESS AND THE POWER,
DRINK BY DRINK, HOUR BY HOUR,
ALL SHALL LOVE ME,
ALL SHALL LOVE ME.

"This makes a very powerful powder," said Agatha. "It grows over time. Every sip of water those children take, the more obsessed with Zak they'll become."

"He said he p-put it on the t-tap." Charlie's forehead was wrinkled as she tried to remember what Zak had told her.

"Yes," said Agatha, "that makes sense. If the jugs are filled from the same source, all he'd have to do was enchant the source."

Charlie nodded. The canteen tap – he'd have chosen that.

"Part of me still can't believe Zak did it." Kat shook her head. "He seemed so nice."

"He might be," said Agatha. "Sometimes we get mixed up in the wrong things and, before we know it, they consume us. And then. . ."

Charlie stared at Agatha. "*Havoc*," she breathed. She remembered what had happened to Eliza now. The more dark magic a witch used, the more havoc would follow: a kind of bad luck that could be fatal. For Eliza, the moment she cast a curse on Suzy, the havoc grew too strong for even Agatha to stop.

"Yes," said Agatha quietly. "Legend goes, it was the Snake Sisters' havoc that brought the Witchfinder General to Broom Hill. The day he arrived, there was a cold chill in the air, an eerie green light."

"But one of the S-Snake Sisters escaped?"

"Havoc caught up with her too. It always does in the end. They say she died not long after, in a freak storm."

"Does . . . does this m-m-mean something bad will happen to Zak?" As annoying as he was, Charlie didn't want that!

"Not necessarily. There may still be time. Zak is young. His powers aren't that strong yet – he's still playing." Agatha's gaze was steady as she looked at Charlie. "It's easy for young witches to go down the path of dark magic. It's hard work, being a witch. Sometimes it's simpler to cast spells from a place of anger or hate than from love."

Charlie blushed. She felt a wave of sympathy for Zak. If she hadn't had someone to guide her, someone like Agatha, she too could have been even more tempted to use dark magic. What if she'd found that book without knowing the dangers?

"We n-n-need to help him!" she said urgently.

"Can't we stop him using dark magic?" Kat said at the same time.

"You can try," Agatha said softly. There was a sadness in her eyes. She sat down in her armchair.

"But it's very hard to *make* someone do something," she said. "Even if you can see that the path they are on is wrong. Even if you know it won't end well, you can't force them on to a different one. The Book of Shadows is very powerful. It lures witches in, promising great things. Before a witch knows it, she's caught . . . controlled by the book." Agatha played with the ragged hem of her skirt. "I couldn't help Eliza, and she was my best friend!"

"Wh-what can we do then?" Charlie asked.

"Don't give up on him," Agatha answered quickly. "Keep reminding him that you are there and you can help him. Try not to blame him; try to remember it's the book doing this, not him."

Kat nodded.

"But for now. . ." Agatha stood. "If Zak won't reverse the possession spell, we'll have to do it ourselves. If we don't, it could cause great harm. Remember what I told you – soon Zak will be all those children can think about."

Charlie shivered, picturing a school of Zak-obsessed zombies.

Agatha cleared a space on her table. "Now, what was in Zak's spell?" she asked. Charlie could tell

Agatha already knew *exactly* what was in the spell, but she humoured her by answering:

"Copper, white vinegar and rue."

"Yes. Copper powder is a strong conductor of magical energy. Vinegar clears the mind, allowing the rue to do its job: conquest and domination."

Charlie scribbled everything down.

"So," said Agatha. "What do we use to stop it?"

Kat broke in. "What stopped the spell for me?" she asked.

"When Charlie called for you and you responded, your bond broke the spell," Agatha told her. "The telepathy cleared your mind and brought Charlie back to you."

"Oh," said Kat. "Then we can't use that method on everyone at school." She glanced at Charlie. "No one has a bond like ours."

Charlie gave her a quick smile, then frowned in concentration, searching her brain for ideas.

"Stop." Agatha took a step towards her. She put her hand on her own chest. "Here," she said. "*Feel* it, don't *think* it."

"We need something strong," said Charlie. "People are hooked on that water. They're obsessed with Zak.

We need something powerful enough to break the addiction."

"Yes." Agatha reached behind her. "Dragonwort," she said, "or *Persicaria bistorta*." She put an odd-shaped root on the table. Charlie picked it up and turned it over in her hands. It was knobbly and twisted. "It's a herb used to stop bleeding," Agatha explained. "It also acts as a potion resistor. It will break the craving for the water instantly and, with it, the attraction to Zak. What next?"

"Something to redirect people's feelings? Put them back the way they were?"

Agatha nodded briskly. "Ginseng," she said as she rummaged for a jar. "It fights adaptation, retuning the balance of emotions."

"Um . . . and something gentle, so people aren't hurt."

"Yep. Camomile." She put it on the table. "The leaves of this plant are soothing and softening. Good, Charlie!" Agatha gave her a rare smile.

"Now what?" asked Kat.

"We grind them up," said Agatha. "Then tomorrow, Charlie, you need to paint the powder on the tap and say a chant, which we'll work on this afternoon. The remedy should work as soon as people drink the water."

Charlie nodded. All at once a wave of tiredness washed over her. She gave a huge yawn.

"Sorry!" she said, rushing to cover her mouth. "I'm exhausted."

Agatha laughed. "Go home and get some sleep," she said. She looked at the window. "I think there's a few hours left before dawn." She blew out a candle. "But I expect you both back here after lunch. Spells don't charm themselves, you know. You need to put the work in."

Charlie smiled to herself. Even though Agatha was tough on them she was very pleased they had her to guide them!

By the end of Sunday, after hours of practice, Charlie and Kat's telepathy had grown even stronger. Now Charlie could think of a number or a colour and Kat could say it out loud.

Charlie had also written a chant to say as they poured the powder into the water, to neutralize the spell. Agatha had pronounced it "Adequate", and given one of her little nods, so Charlie knew it would be OK. It was maybe not the most poetic chant in the world, but it would do the job.

As they parted by Charlie's front door, Kat gave her friend a huge hug.

"See you tomorrow," she said. A ripple of warmth ran through Charlie. She lifted the bottle of healing powder in salute. It was great to have her best friend back!

Chapter Twelve

You Have No Power Here

They'd arranged to get to school early on Monday morning, before any of the other students had arrived. Charlie found Kat in their usual meeting place, right by the school entrance. The familiar's face spread into an excited grin when she saw the witch, and Charlie took her arm.

"Come on," she said. "Let's go to the canteen before everyone gets here."

In the canteen, Kat stood guard by the doorway while Charlie slipped through the door next to the counter, the one that opened on to the main bit of the kitchen. On the left there was a large sink. Charlie leaned over the tap. She rubbed the powder on the edge and up inside the spout.

"Ready!" she called.

Kat closed her eyes.

From across the room Charlie could feel the familiar filling her with warmth and energy. A soft tingle passed through her body and she began to chant:

"Stop. Undo.
Reverse. Go Back.
Let water flow,
Resist attack."

There was a shimmer of heat and the tap sparkled for a brief second.

"Here goes. . ." Charlie ran the water and bent her head down to take a quick sip.

"Yep!" she lifted her head with a smile. "It's clear! It tastes like normal water."

Charlie could hardly concentrate all through lessons that morning, desperate to see what would happen. At lunchtime Charlie and Kat hovered at the edge of the canteen, watching to see if the potion would do its work.

They didn't have to wait long. It was astounding

to see the change in mood. Agatha was right – the dragonwort did work instantly. It was as though people had just woken up. They rubbed their eyes and tried to remember what it was they had ever liked about Zak Crawford.

"He's really annoying!" Charlie overheard a girl saying as she walked by. "He shoved past me to get to the water fountain."

"I know," said the girl's friend. "I never liked him. At least, I don't *think* I did."

Charlie felt the building relax. By the afternoon there was a happy contentment in the air and people went back to normal, chatting about Halloween and the eclipse that coming weekend: parties were arranged and costume ideas were swapped. For once, no one argued over Zak. No one sniped over whose house he was hanging out at more or who got to carry his bag. Charlie smiled to herself as she walked through the corridor. The school felt . . . what was it?

Free.

"What are you wearing for Halloween?" Kat caught her arm after the final bell. "I can't wait! Let's do trick or treating first, then go and see Agatha."

A thrill ran through Charlie. In all the excitement she'd nearly forgotten – Samhain! Her first as a witch! Yes – on Saturday night, at Samhain, together she and Kat would say a special chant to help the village. They would hang their blessing wreaths, and welcome in the new year.

Just then, Charlie sensed a coldness. Zak was marching down the hall towards them, his face set in a scowl. Charlie shuddered as he glared at her. An icy wave washed over her from head to toe.

"You broke my spell!" he snarled. "And you *must* have looked in your Book of Shadows to find a counter-spell." He scoffed bitterly. "After all you said about not using dark magic! Not so high and mighty now, are we, *Banana*?"

Charlie felt a hand on her arm: Kat. "She only used the Book of Shadows to find out what spell you had cast," said the familiar calmly. "She wrote the counter-spell herself."

Zak's mouth opened in amazement.

"How?" he said eventually.

"I told you," Charlie said. "Kat m-makes my magic stronger."

Zak looked from Charlie to Kat.

"A familiar made you *that* strong?"

"Together we can do anything," Kat said proudly.

A look of envy flashed across Zak's face. He breathed in and closed his eyes for a moment. The three of them stood there, letting the other students rush past them out of school. Soon the corridor was nearly empty.

"Funny how none of them know anything." Zak jerked his head at the last few pupils.

Charlie nodded. She knew what he meant.

"For a while I thought it was just me who knew all these secrets," Zak continued, "and now it seems there's three of us. Three musketeers. . . Well . . . two musketeers and me."

Kat winced in sympathy.

"You're lucky, you two," said Zak. "I'd love to know there was someone on my side."

Charlie remembered what Agatha said: *Try not to blame Zak . . . it's the book doing this, not him.* They were supposed to be helping him.

"Why d-don't you come and meet Agatha," she suggested.

"Who's Agatha?"

"She's a witch. She's tr-training us: Kat and me. She knows so m-much! She's got *years* of experience!"

"Uh, no thanks," said Zak. The arrogant tone to his voice crept back in. "I don't need some old lady telling me what to do." He snorted. "*You* might need training, but I don't. I already know how to use magic. It's easy. I just think about things that make me cross and *pow*! I can do stuff!"

Charlie shook her head. "That's dark magic – and it's dangerous," she tried to explain. "Y-you have to l-l-learn to use your power properly. You can't t-trust a Book of Shadows to t-teach you."

Zak snorted.

"R-r-really," Charlie insisted. Her words were beginning to congeal inside her; they felt stodgy and gloopy. "That b-book – it used to b-belong to a d-d-dark witch. It s-s-started to control her, and it l-led to her death!"

"Huh. Well. Maybe she wasn't strong enough to use it properly. I am."

"You have to st-st-stop." Charlie looked at Kat for help. "Dark magic is dangerous – it brings bad luck. Really bad luck. It's called havoc—"

Zak laughed, "Ooh, *bad luck*. Now I'm *sooo* scared," he said sarcastically. "Come on, Banana – is that the best you've got? Look..." He held up his hands. "I know you mean well but I told you – I'm fine. I won't let it *control* me. All right? And I promise I won't do any more mind tricks on the school, if that's what you're worried about."

"Why don't you have lunch with us tomorrow?" Kat said gently.

Zak shrugged.

"All right," he said, at last. "I might ask you more about this familiar thing."

That night at the cottage, Agatha toasted them with a cup of ginseng tea. "That possession spell was a tricky one to reverse," she said. "You did well." She gave one of her little nods.

But Charlie was still worried.

"We invited Zak to the c-cottage," she said, "but he d-didn't want to come."

"Give him time," Agatha said.

"We're having lunch with him tomorrow," Kat added.

"That's good. You two are the best placed to help.

But I fear it might be a long road ahead for him. He has to *want* to put that book down. And that won't be easy."

Later, as Kat was inside practising with the scrying mirror, Charlie went outside with Agatha and sat down on the grass.

"How do w-w-witches get a familiar?" she asked, thinking of Zak.

"Not every witch does," Agatha answered. She sat down opposite Charlie, on the stone doorstep. "Many go through the whole of their magic lives without finding one."

"Have you g-g-got one?"

"I did have. A long time ago."

Charlie waited to hear.

"Cora. She was Hopfoot's mother. One day, many years ago, I was sitting by the stream, trying to cast a healing spell, when I heard a noise. A crow was sitting on the branch above me. She was looking at me strangely and . . . I can't explain it . . . I just knew we were connected."

Charlie nodded. She recognized what Agatha was describing. Ever since she'd met Kat, she'd felt a thread linking them, a kind of bond.

"Cora stayed with me for a long time. She was my friend, my energy, my light."

"What h-happened to her?" Charlie hardly dared ask.

Agatha looked down. She picked a little daisy by her feet. "We took on something too big." Her voice trembled. "Do you remember I told you how I tried to break the curse on Suzy Evans?"

Charlie nodded. Eliza had bound the curse with the phrase: "No witch alive can break my spell."

But Agatha had tried anyway.

"It cost me my little finger," said Agatha. "But I lost something much, much worse. I lost my familiar."

The witch's voice shook and a tear trickled down her cheek.

"It was my fault. I shouldn't have tried to break the curse. But I was desperate. Cora and I were so strong together. I thought I could do it. I thought I could fix everything. But I couldn't." Her voice was croaky. "In the end I had lost Eliza and Cora." She shook her head helplessly.

Charlie's throat was dry. She didn't know what to say.

"From that day on," said Agatha, "I hid away in my cottage hardly seeing anyone. I was here for seventeen years. . ." She spun the daisy round and round in her fingers. "Until you came, Charlie." Agatha lifted her head. A calmness settled over her face.

Charlie thought of something:

"Couldn't Hopfoot be your f-f-familiar, if he's Cora's son?"

"It doesn't work like that." Agatha shook her head. "You can't manufacture a familiar. The bond has to be there naturally. Come on," she said, her voice deliberately casual, "let's see how Kat is getting on."

Agatha opened the door slowly.

Kat was sitting in the centre of the rug. She shook her head when she saw Agatha.

"I can't quite see anything," she said. "There's a kind of swirling, a mist inside the obsidian, but I can't make out any shapes."

"You will soon," answered Agatha cryptically. "With a little help."

All the way home, Charlie thought about what Agatha had said earlier, about losing Cora. She couldn't bear the thought of anything happening to Kat! She'd feel empty inside, half a witch without her friend. Kat made her so much stronger, so much more powerful. She made Charlie feel as though she could do anything – as if even her stutter couldn't hold her back. Her thoughts flitted to Zak. *I'd love to know there was someone on my side*, he'd said. Charlie felt a twinge of sympathy for him. It must be hard to go through all this alone, to have to learn about magic yourself, from a book. She resolved to be nicer to him. Starting with lunch tomorrow.

Chapter Thirteen
Season of the Witch

On Tuesday, for the first time, Zak, Charlie and Kat ate lunch together. They sat out on the grass. It was cold, but that meant there were fewer people around to hear them.

It was kind of nice, Charlie had to admit, getting to talk about secret witch stuff with someone else her own age. Charlie told Zak all about Suzy Evans, the star of the school – how she'd been under a curse and hadn't even known it.

"And you and Kat managed to break it?" Zak sounded impressed.

"Yep!" said Kat with a grin.

"Together we're s-s-so much more powerful," Charlie said with pride.

"What does it feel like?" Zak asked. "Working together?"

"It's like a thread," Charlie tried to explain. "When we're two I can *feel* Kat – s-sense what she's doing. When I'm t-tired, she helps. She sends me energy, warmth."

Kat nodded in enthusiasm. "We're getting stronger too," she said in excitement. "We can do telepathy!"

"Go on then. Let's see!" Zak said eagerly.

Charlie had a sudden desire to show Zak how strong she was when she was with Kat. She was proud of her friend and proud of herself. Besides, she told herself, maybe this would make it clear to Zak how powerful white magic could be.

She sat opposite Kat and closed her eyes. Zak whispered a colour into Kat's ear and Charlie focused hard to tune into Kat's thoughts. She breathed deeper and deeper, settling down into the world she shared with Kat, following the thread of magic until she was in Kat's head.

"Purple," she said out loud, and opened her eyes.

"That's pretty cool," said Zak, rubbing the back of his neck. "Do it again."

This time Zak whispered a number in to Charlie's ear and it was Kat who had to guess. Charlie was reaching out to her, sending thoughts of 347.29 across the grass, when she felt something funny. There was someone pushing in. It was a bit like when she heard Matt eavesdropping on the landline. Like an extra presence, an extra breath, an extra ghost of someone. She opened her eyes fast. Zak had copied Charlie's pose and was sitting cross-legged on the ground with his eyes shut.

"Hey!" cried Charlie and she broke the connection.

Zak held up his hands in defence. "I was just curious. For the record, I couldn't get in, you know. You have something, the pair of you, and I couldn't break into it."

Charlie breathed out slowly, relieved.

"It's amazing, what you two can do," Zak said, his tone genuinely awed. "I see what you mean now about white magic being powerful. How did you find each other? I'd love a familiar to practise with."

"I don't know how you find one," Kat answered. "Do you, Charlie?"

Charlie looked at Zak. He was looking back at her,

interested and open. She remembered what Agatha had said – *Don't give up on him. Keep reminding him that you are there and you can help him.*

She tried to explain it as Agatha had put it. "You see someone – a p-person or an, an animal – and you just know you are c-connected. . ." She trailed off. It was so hard to describe!

Zak brow furrowed in confusion. "I don't get it."

Kat answered this time. "When you see them, you know instantly that they are a missing part of you, as if without them you wouldn't be complete." Charlie nodded quickly. That was exactly what it was like.

Zak looked down and was quiet for a moment. "I've never felt like that about someone," he said slowly. "But. . ." He looked suddenly nervous. ". . . I-I've felt that there's a part of *me* that's different. I mean. . ." He frowned and bit his lip. "A part that's not like the rest of me."

"Go on," said Kat gently.

"Like sometimes, my mind goes a bit fuzzy and then the world looks weird for a moment – I'm out of my body; I'm a different creature. Like I'm running or jumping or even flying!" he added with a little laugh. He looked down and played with a bit of dry grass.

"I d-don't know what that m-means," Charlie said, "but Agatha would know."

Zak screwed up his face in frustration. "I'm sure I haven't properly tapped into my power yet. I know I have more; I just can't seem to get to it." His voice was tense.

The bell rang for the end of lunch.

"Why don't you come and train with us this afternoon?" suggested Kat kindly. "I'm sure Agatha will have the answers to some of this."

"Maybe I will," Zak answered.

But when the afternoon bell went, Zak wasn't at the meeting place. Kat and Charlie waited a few extra minutes just in case but. . .

"He's not coming," Kat said.

At Agatha's, even though Zak wasn't there with them in person, to Charlie's annoyance, he was there with them in spirit. Every time Charlie and Kat tried telepathy one of them would think about Zak. They couldn't stop themselves. It was like he had got inside their minds.

First, in her head, Charlie saw him going into Moonquest, the new-age shop in town. In Charlie's vision she caught a flash of Zak buying a thin leather cord.

She pulled out of the trance and shook her head to get rid of him.

Then Kat saw him too.

"He was carving something on the leather!" she cried. "He had a teeny knife." Kat opened and closed her eyes, as if she was trying to push the image from her head.

"What's he d-doing? And wh-why is he in our heads?" Charlie moaned to Agatha.

The witch was standing by the window, looking up at the sky.

"I don't know what he's doing. But I think I know why he keeps entering your thoughts." She turned from the window. "Did you say you showed Zak your telepathy?" she asked.

"Yes – and he tried to push in. . ."

"That's it, then. You and he share a bond now. And remember, you were both already very strongly connected to him," she went on. "Kat, the charmed water made you drawn to him, and

Charlie, you and he shared the experience of dark magic."

"Will it pass?" asked Kat. "It's driving me mad!"

"It will," said Agatha. "In time. But for now, well, it has its uses."

"What do you m-mean?" Charlie wanted to know.

"Don't worry about that at the moment." Agatha waved her hand, making it clear that, for her, the subject was closed. "Let's focus on Samhain. Charlie – I want you to write the chant."

"By myself?"

"Yes. You're ready, I'm sure. Your chant to reverse the possession spell worked well."

"But. . ." Charlie began. "It's on Saturday . . . that's only four days away."

Agatha smiled at her gently. "Just start with your wreath," she said. "Think about what you want to say while you plait."

"I'll work on mine too," said Kat.

There was silence for a while as they wove the twigs in and out of each other. Charlie looked up.

Agatha was standing by the window. Her shoulders were tense, the dress fabric taut over her back.

"Are you all right?" Charlie asked.

"Uh-huh," she said, distracted.

"Agatha?" Charlie used a louder voice and this time the witch turned.

"Oh! Sorry!" She tucked her long black hair behind her ears. "I was just watching for Hopfoot. He's normally here by now."

Charlie joined her at the window. Agatha was right. Hopfoot usually arrived at half past three like clockwork, for a stroke, a nibble to eat and a chat.

Charlie frowned. "I'm sure he'll turn up soon," she said. "He's p-probably sitting on a b-branch in the sun somewhere."

Agatha nodded. She took a final look out the window and then clapped her hands once lightly, shaking herself out of the mood.

"Wreaths!" she said in an overly cheerful voice.

Charlie picked hers up again and brought it on to the rug. She remembered what Agatha had said – think about what you want to achieve in the year to come.

She flicked through her file of herbs, selecting those that brought friendship and peace: lavender flowers, cloves, basil and rosemary. She crushed them in Agatha's pestle and mortar until they were a fine paste. Then she bound them with sweet pea oil and brushed the honeysuckle vine with the mixture.

"Mmm, that smells good!" Kat breathed in. "Can I put some of that on my wreath too?" Charlie handed her the brush. Kat had drawn markings on her vine; there was a cat leaping and a ring of circles that spun round and round in a never-ending loop.

"I like that one!" Charlie pointed to the loop.

"I got it from your file." Kat showed her. Underneath the image of the loop it said:

TO INCREASE THE BOND OF FRIENDSHIP.

Charlie smiled at the familiar. "I'm going to put th-that on my wreath too," she said.

By dinnertime both blessing wreaths were finished, and they smelled amazing – warm and spicy and sweet.

"We'll hang them up on Saturday," said Agatha.

Charlie arrived home just in time to set the table for dinner. Matt swept in, still wearing green face paint from rehearsal.

"How's the p-play going?" she asked.

"Great!" Matt stole one of Dad's home-made chips while he wasn't looking. "We look like real witches.

It's so cool! You'll see on Monday."

"Yeah?" Charlie kept her voice light.

"We've got dry ice and these black cloaks and everything!"

"And. . ." Charlie gestured to her face. "Anything else? Are you feeling OK, Matt? You're looking a little . . . green!"

"Oh, yeah! Face paint. I'd better take this off before dinner." Matt rushed upstairs. Charlie grinned and shook her head.

"Wa-ha-ha-ha!" she could hear him cackling at Annie, and Annie cackling back. Annie was so excited about Halloween. She asked every morning if it was time to put on the costume Charlie had made her. Every morning Charlie told her it was on Saturday. Four sleeps to go.

Four sleeps for Charlie too, before Samhain.

Chapter Fourteen

Flying Monkeys

Charlie was running through the forest, bounding at top speed. She wasn't sure how her legs were moving so quickly, but then she looked down and saw that instead of feet, she was running on four hairy paws equipped with razor-sharp claws. She tore through the undergrowth, feeling the grass on her furry tummy as she ran. She came to a log and she leapt. All at once her back legs changed. Now she was a hare bouncing lightly from rock to rock on a mountain, up, up, to the very top. She jumped to the edge and off, floating down with the wings of an eagle. As she soared through the air, her heart lifted and a wave of happiness bubbled up inside her. She felt free and at home.

Down on the grass below, her beady eyes caught sight of movement: a small creature was darting about. A mouse! She held her sharp talons out before her, ready to pounce on the prey. She twitched her beak at the thought of the delicious little creature below her, warm with flowing blood. She hit the ground and she was human again, but she wasn't Charlie: she was Zak.

Charlie sat up, gasping. Her heart was thumping and her mouth felt dry. Another dream. She wriggled her back to shake off the feeling of wings. It had seemed so real! In the moonlight, she turned her hands over, checking for fur or claws.

She lay back down, trying to calm her beating heart and clear her thoughts. Ever since they had shown Zak their telepathy Charlie could feel him creeping in. He was there at the edge of her thoughts. Tonight had been worst of all: she had shared Zak's mind. And how strange it was! Zak dreamed about animals so realistically. It couldn't even be called a dream *about* animals, Charlie corrected herself; in Zak's dreams he *was* an animal. He experienced the world as they did, sharing their abilities and their desires. Charlie had never felt anything like it.

Charlie lay awake for a while afterwards, thinking.

At school on Wednesday Charlie felt strangely embarrassed at the thought of seeing Zak. Would he know they'd shared a dream? Should she tell him how strange it had felt? She hadn't meant to see into his head. How had it even happened?

"Are you OK?" Kat found her in the corridor. Her forehead wrinkled as she studied Charlie.

"Yeah," Charlie nodded. "I just had a weird d-dream last night."

Charlie told Kat all about it.

Kat shuddered when she heard about the field mouse.

"It was actually amazing." Charlie rubbed her forehead. "It was so vivid, so real. In Zak's dreams he can f-feel exactly what it's like being up in the cl-clouds."

Kat nudged Charlie. Zak was at his locker. These days there was no one hanging around it, but Zak didn't seem to mind at all. He opened it and swapped his books over.

Kat tilted her head to the side.

"He's glowing," she said slowly. "He has a kind of cold, green light."

Charlie watched him closely. Kat was right. There was a chill in the air around him, a slight tingle of dark magic. . .

"What are you up to, Z-Z-Zak?" Charlie asked, walking towards him.

Zak grinned and tapped the side of his nose. There was a strange gleam in his eye. "Nothing for you to worry about."

"Don't use d-d-dark magic," said Charlie. "Please."

"It's not safe," Kat added. "We told you about havoc—"

"I'll. Be. Fine." He said each word clearly.

Then he made his hands into little mouths and made them open and close.

"Careful, Zak!" whined one hand. "Stop it, Zaaaak!" whined the other. He winked at the two of them.

"Chill out," he said with a grin. "I'm just trying something. And it'll blow you away, I promise."

"Then I w-was an eagle, then Z-Zak again." Charlie was telling Agatha about the weird dream.

The witch was quiet, but Charlie could see her mind ticking over.

"What d-d-does it mean?"

Agatha waved her hand in the air vaguely as if she didn't know, or, at least, didn't want to say.

Something else was bothering Charlie.

"If . . . I got into Z-Z-Zak's head. . ." She paused and twisted her fingers in and out of each other. ". . . Does that m-mean I've done s-s-something wrong?"

"No, Charlie," Agatha soothed her. "You didn't use dark magic to get in there. You didn't force your way in. In your sleep you were relaxed, so the connection you share with him blossomed. That's how it happened."

"I didn't w-w-want to be there!" Charlie was desperate to explain.

"It's OK," Agatha said, reassuringly. "I know you didn't."

"And now I can sense him even m-more." Charlie frowned. "And he is up to s-s-something, I know it."

"Come." Agatha clapped her hands. "Practise!" She stood up and brushed imaginary dust off her long dress.

"Bu-but. . ."

Agatha set her jaw. "The best way to face dark magic is to be strong enough to deal with it," she said firmly. "Charlie, you need to learn to move that stone, and Kat, I want you to try again with the scrying mirror. We may need it soon. And you still need to write your chant, Charlie. I want the blessing ritual to be extra strong this year."

Charlie looked up at that, but Agatha refused to meet her eyes. Instead, she took a quick glance out of the window.

"Still no Hopfoot?" Charlie guessed.

"I haven't seen him since yesterday morning." Agatha frowned. "He even missed lunch today."

"That's not like him," said Kat.

"No," said Agatha in a quiet voice. "It's not." She cleared her throat. "Right. Come on, then."

All afternoon they practised.

Kat was slowly getting there with the scrying mirror. She could now see figures in the mist. But she couldn't tell who they were.

"They're just fuzzy!" she complained. "I can't focus on them."

But Agatha smiled as if the familiar had done well.

Charlie worked hard on her telekinesis. She had to move the stone with her mind, this time without exploding it. She calmed herself and focused in on warmth – on nature and creation. She probed the stone gently, trying to find its essence. She felt its hardness, its smoothness, and sensed the passage of time that had brought it there. She imagined it moving, rolling, shifting on the grass. All at once she felt it give. She opened her eyes – the stone had rolled! It was lying to the side of her now.

"Good job, Charlie," said Agatha softly. Her eyes shone with pride. Then her tone turned serious. "I need you to try something," she told the girls. They looked up at her. "It concerns Zak," the witch continued. "You already have a strong telepathic link with him. Now, I want you to find him in your minds, and follow him. Exploit that link to find out what he is up to. Together you should be strong enough to watch what he is doing right now."

"You mean . . . spy on him?" Kat was hesitant.

Agatha took time to choose her words. "Normally I would never use power to spy on someone. People's lives are private. But. . ." She paused for a moment and then carried on. "That boy is headed down a very dangerous path indeed. And we need to do everything we can to stop him." Her voice hardened. "I will NOT lose another witch to dark magic," she said firmly.

Charlie and Kat nodded. They would help.

Charlie closed her eyes and felt for the thread that bound her and Kat, and then her and Zak. She could feel Kat reaching out too. She heard Agatha's voice, as if from far away:

"Just relax. Let your mind drift away; follow wherever it goes."

Charlie felt her mind merge with Kat. Warmth filled her body. Together they hovered, waiting to see where their thoughts would take them.

A cold vision filled her head – a cage.

She frowned and shrank back from it.

"Follow your thoughts." Agatha's voice was insistent, pushing the girls onwards.

Charlie let her mind go and plunged into the shared world. The cage was back. There was a bird inside it. The image was blurry, like a photo out of focus.

"Come on. I want to see what you can do," said a voice.

Zak! Charlie gasped. Agatha placed a hand on her head to calm her.

Charlie watched as Zak opened the door of the cage. The bird came closer and the image sharpened. It was Hopfoot! Kat cried out and Charlie reached for her hand. The girls watched as Zak wrapped something thin and brown around Hopfoot's leg.

"Go!" he cried.

Hoptfoot flew up into the air.

Zak lay back on the brown grass. He closed his eyes and smiled.

Hopfoot stumbled in the air. Side to side he weaved, as if he was drunk. He flew towards the forest, towards Agatha's cottage in little jerks, confused and uncertain. Then he seemed to stop in mid-air, as if he had forgotten how to fly. Down he fell, towards the earth below.

Charlie and Kat opened their eyes at once.

"Hopfoot!" Charlie cried.

"He's hurt!" Kat said at the same time.

"Go!" cried Agatha. "Find him."

Together they rushed out of Agatha's garden and into the woods.

"Hopfoot!" Kat cupped her hands around her mouth and yelled, over and over again.

Charlie listened for a response. Nothing.

They tried another direction, Kat calling and Charlie listening. Nothing . . . nothing. . .

"Wait!" Charlie held up her hand. There it was: a soft *caw!* "This way!" she cried and they ran towards the sound.

Caw!

Caw!

They were closer now. Hopfoot was somewhere nearby, in the thickest part of the woods. Charlie and Kat fought their way through the dry undergrowth and tree roots.

Caw!

Charlie caught a flash of black against the red leaves.

"Here!" she cried. She fell down beside the fallen bird.

"Oh, Hopfoot!" Kat's voice was choked.

They stared at the little body before them. The crow was panting shallow breaths of exhaustion.

His feathers were torn in places and he held one of his legs at an awkward angle.

Kat gathered him up with tears in her eyes, too shocked and upset to speak. Charlie parted the brambles for her as Kat carried the injured bird home to Agatha.

"Allspice, b-bay and eucalyptus." Charlie chose the best healing herbs. Agatha handed her the ingredients and Charlie quickly mashed everything together into a paste. She dipped a bandage into the mixture and wrapped it around Hopfoot as gently as she could.

Kat sat in the armchair, watching with tears running down her cheeks.

Charlie rested her hands on Hopfoot's feathers. Her fingers stroked him, trying to stop him shaking. As she passed along his body, she felt a bump. She looked down: on his leg was a little cord of leather tied in a knot. She peered closer. It had markings: scratches on the leather.

"Wh-what's this?"

Agatha looked down. Her face went white and she clenched her fists then snapped the cord off.

"It's a lock-circle," she said through gritted teeth. "It forces a bond between people and animals."

"Zak." Charlie breathed. "He's been desperate for a familiar. He must have tried to make Hopfoot his."

"There, there," Agatha crooned to the crow. "The tie is broken now. Just rest."

The bird gave a soft *chirrup* and his feathers relaxed as he fell asleep.

Chapter Fifteen
Howlet's Wing

Charlie slept badly that night. She kept thinking about Hopfoot's little body, lying there under the bandage. She'd stroked him over and over, and said a healing chant. Then Agatha had tucked a soft comfrey leaf around him "to keep the swelling down". Now all they could do was hope he'd get better soon.

At school, Kat was waiting. Charlie had never seen her so angry.

"Where is he?" she snarled.

They found Zak outside the music corridor.

"How could you?!" Kat's green eyes were dark as she glared at Zak.

Zak stepped back at the sight of her. He looked uncertain.

"How could you hurt Hopfoot?" Even though Kat was smaller than him, Zak shrank from the anger in her voice.

"Wh-who's Hopfoot?" he stammered.

Kat folded her arms and looked at Charlie helplessly. She was too furious to speak. For once it was Charlie who had all the words.

"Hopfoot is our friend." Her voice was clear and cold. "You forced yourself into his mind and you hurt him."

"The crow?" Zak was puzzled.

"Yes." Charlie nodded.

"Oh!" Zak sounded genuinely shocked. "I didn't know he was your friend! I just thought he was an old crow."

Kat spluttered in anger.

"You shouldn't hurt *any* of the crows." Charlie's voice was like ice. "Poor Hopfoot is lying in Agatha's cottage, injured. You could have broken his leg!"

"I'm sorry, OK!" Zak ran his hand through his hair. His face looked tired and there were shadows under his eyes. "I just. . . I wanted. . . I needed to feel like I was flying. I can't explain it. You'd have to be there to know what it's like."

A flush spread over Charlie as her dream came flooding back. She caught Kat's eye and turned away before Zak could see her bright red face.

"You two, you're all sorted . . . but me. . ." Zak sounded small. "I'm a bit of a mess," he admitted.

"We t-told you not to use dark magic," Charlie muttered. "It's dangerous."

"I know," Zak admitted. "I just didn't think—"

"That's the problem isn't it?" snapped Kat, still furious. "You didn't think!"

At this, Zak lost his temper. "You two reckon you're so great, don't you?" he said angrily. "Stop telling me what to do! I don't tell you how to use your powers; why is it OK to tell me how to use mine?"

"You are *hurting* creatures," Kat said. "That's the difference!"

"Oh yeah! Well, what about *me*?" Zak growled. "What about how *I* feel? You've got each other and I'm on my own. I want a familiar too. . . I . . . I keep having these dreams and I don't know what's wrong."

"Then c-c-come to see Agatha with us," Charlie said. She tried to keep her voice reasonable, to calm things down.

"No way! I know what she'll say – stop using the book, don't use dark magic. Just because I made one little mistake, none of you think I can handle it. Well, I can. At least I could if you two stopped interfering. Just leave me alone." He paused, breathing heavily. "And you don't have to worry – I won't use magic on any living creature again." He stopped abruptly, his eyes narrowing suddenly. "On any living creature. . ." he repeated.

"Zak. . ." Charlie tried again.

"Stop it!" he snapped. "Just leave me alone, like I said. I don't need you." And he stormed off down the corridor.

After school, Charlie and Kat rushed to the cottage to see Hopfoot.

When they got there they found the bird perched on Agatha's lap. She was feeding him nuts.

"Your healing chant worked, Charlie." Agatha's face was tired but Charlie could see the relief in her eyes.

"I'm glad." Charlie smiled weakly.

Kat took over from Agatha, holding the crow gently, like a baby. "Hey, gorgeous!" she crooned in her low Welsh voice. Hopfoot gingerly held out his head to be patted. As he did, Charlie caught his eye. She smiled at him and, under Kat's fingers, he nodded gently.

"Hopfoot helped me," Charlie told Agatha as Kat gave him all her attention. "One n-night when the book was c-calling to me, I nearly gave in. But he s-stopped me."

Agatha tilted her head. "That crow is very wise, like his mother. Now, girls," she said, and her voice was grave. "I need you to watch Zak carefully tomorrow. I fear this attempt to control Hopfoot won't be the last thing he'll try."

At school on Friday, Charlie and Kat were on Zak-watch. Well, at least they would have been if they could have found him. But he was nowhere to be seen.

By lunchtime there was still no sign of him anywhere. Charlie and Kat split up to search in and out of the rooms, the corridors and the gym. Charlie was just heading down the art corridor when she saw Kat waving from the door of the library.

"He's in here!" Kat mouthed.

Charlie breathed out in relief.

Together they opened the door to the library and Kat led the way between the aisles of books. She put her hand on Charlie's arm and pointed in between the shelves to the row parallel. Together they peeped through at Zak.

He was sitting on the floor in the history section. He was surrounded by books all about the town. *Famous Town Landmarks* was by his knee, *The Broomwood Wolf and Other Myths and Legends* was by his foot, and *A History of Broomwood* was open on his lap.

Charlie looked at Kat. *What is he up to?* She asked with her eyebrows.

Kat shrugged her answer.

Suddenly Zak hit a page with his finger and gave a triumphant little cry. An icy buzz hit Charlie and Kat shielded her eyes from the glow. They shrank back behind a shelf as Zak rushed out of the library.

Charlie ran to the next row and picked up the book Zak had dropped – *A History of Broomwood.*

"What did he f-find in here?" she wondered aloud, scanning the pages he'd been looking at. There were some old photos of Broomwood; here was the village well, and a sketch of the Spindle pub from the 1800s. Charlie couldn't see anything witch-like. In the middle of the page were aerial photos of the village. It looked teeny from above! There was an odd shape in one of the photos, a kind of pattern in the ground – almost like a star. Charlie couldn't work out what it was.

"I don't know what he found," said Kat, looking over Charlie's shoulder, "but whatever it was, he seemed pretty pleased."

Charlie swallowed. That's what she was worried about.

Chapter Sixteen
Look to the Western Skies

They set out all their worries before Agatha, finishing with Zak's mysterious discovery in the library.

"He was b-b-buzzing with dark magic!" Charlie cried, her face pale with the memory of it.

"And he had a horrible glow," added Kat. "It was like a cold green light."

"Wh-what's he doing?" Charlie wanted to know. "He w-wants a familiar. He says he wants to fly. . . He w-wants more power. . ." She bit her lip. "There could be all k-kinds of awful spells in that Book of Shadows!"

Agatha pursed her mouth. "I can think of lots of things he could be doing . . . and not one of them is good." She paced back and forth before the fire. Her hands twisted in and out of each other and her dark purple eyes studied the floor as she walked. Charlie had never seen her so concerned.

Soon she stopped moving.

"I told you before that Samhain is the start of the new year for witches," she said, her voice steady. "It's also the time when we honour those who have died, paying respect to their souls in the Otherworld. The veil between the world of the living and the Otherworld is at its thinnest on the night of the thirty-first of October, and it's a time when dark magic is strong. You will feel it in the air around you."

Charlie listened, an uneasy feeling growing inside her.

"This year, Samhain coincides with a lunar eclipse, a blood moon eclipse as some call it. In the witch calendar, the lunar eclipse is a time of change and uncertainty. Because of this, the spells we cast on Saturday night will be stronger but also more chaotic, harder to control. You and Kat have been training hard to be ready, but Zak..." She paused. Her eyes were filled with anxiety. "Zak, I worry about. It would be very easy for a new witch to be led down the wrong path at Samhain, to take a route he can't come back from."

Charlie swallowed.

Agatha sighed softly. "I need you to try something." She looked at both her students one by one. "It will be hard. But Zak needs our help."

Charlie gripped one hand tight with the other. Next to her she could feel Kat rising on to her tiptoes with tension. They waited to hear.

"The Book of Shadows wants to be used. It knows Samhain is its best chance to pull Zak in, to tempt him to become a dark witch. It will be calling him to cast a spell tomorrow night, when dark magic is strongest. We need to know what that spell will be. . . You've both done so well with your telepathy, and, Kat, I know how hard you've been practising with the scrying mirror. . ."

"I can't use it properly," Kat burst out in a panic. "I can't see the future!"

"Not without Charlie you can't, no," Agatha answered gently. "But together . . . well, I think there's something we should try."

The girls had lots of questions but Agatha shook her head. "Places, please!" she said firmly.

Charlie sat down opposite Kat. Agatha placed the scrying mirror between them.

"Now, Kat, tell Charlie what it feels like to look in the mirror."

Kat thought about it.

"It looks like solid black stone at first," she said slowly. "And then . . . then you focus on it so much you kind of see through it, inside it." She frowned. "It's like you slip into it; you fall. Then there's mist, lots of deep foggy mist." She looked up at Agatha. "I sometimes see shapes but nothing proper."

"That's fine," Agatha said briskly. "Charlie – your job is to follow Kat into the mirror. Concentrate hard on sharing her thoughts. Kat, your talent can get you both into the mirror, but you need a witch to interpret what's there."

"Wh-what am I looking for?" asked Charlie.

"Discord, uncertainty, darkness – anything that doesn't feel right. Feel for it. You'll know it when you sense it."

Charlie nodded.

"Reading the future isn't easy." She addressed them both. "I've never been able to do it, but, from what my mother said, it's not like seeing an exact vision of what's to come; it's more like a puzzle, a series of shapes and pictures we have to put together."

Charlie swallowed. Her fingers were trembling and she laced them together so Kat didn't see.

"Focus on Samhain, tomorrow night," Agatha directed. "Imagine the red moon, the bright stars. Feel the warmth of the earth and the magic all around you."

Charlie closed her eyes. She focused in on her familiar, catching the thread that joined them together. There! She saw the mirror through Kat's eyes. At first it looked black and solid but, together, they plunged towards it, and Charlie felt the volcanic glass melt into a soft fog. She reached for Kat's hand and held it tight.

It was dark. A swirling mist surrounded them. Charlie looked up to see hundreds of stars winking and, behind her, a blood-red moon.

"The eclipse," she murmured. Kat's fingers tightened around hers.

Charlie heard a low chanting in the distance. Suddenly there was a whoosh of air. The wind whipped them up into the sky and they were floating high above the land. Down below them Charlie could make out a shape on a hill: it was a pattern, an outline made of dark patches. She frowned. She'd seen it before. But she didn't have time to think it through.

The fog swirled and now they were back on the muddy ground, looking at a boy – Zak. He was covered in markings, his skin criss-crossed with drawings in red and green and yellow. Candles surrounded him, flickering light and shadow, light and shadow.

Zak knelt with his arms outstretched. A jet-black book lay before him on the earth. In an eerie voice he chanted:

"WIND BLOW,
SPIRIT FREE.
I CALL TO YOU,
COME TO ME."

There was a swirl of cold green light. It surrounded Zak, spinning around him faster and faster. Charlie felt an icy current run through her, the jolt of dark magic. It prickled at her bones like thousands of needles.

"Stop!" she shouted. She reached out her arms, but her fingers grasped at nothing. Her feet sank into the mud and she fell.

Chapter Seventeen
A Ghost of a Chance

Charlie's eyes shot open in fear. A scream caught in her throat. . . But there – there was the armchair, the hanging herbs, the warm fire. She was back – back on Agatha's rug, in Agatha's cottage.

She sat up, shaking and pale.

Kat's face was white, her hand covering her mouth.

"What did you see?" Agatha's voice was urgent and pressing.

"I . . . I don't kn-know." Charlie tried to explain it. "The m-moon was r-r-red. Zak was s-s-s-somewhere. He had the Book of Shadows. His arms were up l-l-like this" – Charlie held hers high – "and he was chanting."

"Can you remember what he said?" Agatha broke in quickly.

Charlie nodded. She reached for her file to write down the spell before she forgot it. Agatha breathed in fast when she saw Charlie's words. Something flashed in her eyes.

"He had m-m-markings on his skin." Charlie drew them out for Agatha to see.

"Sigils," said Agatha. She gripped the mantelpiece. "That's a spirit-summoning spell. I was afraid he was going to try something like that."

Charlie's mouth went dry. She stared at Agatha, waiting to hear.

"I think Zak is going to try to conjure up a familiar," the witch said gravely.

"Wh-wh. . ." Charlie couldn't even finish her question.

Agatha explained. "When someone dies they leave us in body, but the earth still holds some of their essence – their memory. Sometimes we catch sight of someone who looks like them or hear a laugh that sounds like theirs."

Charlie nodded. Her grandma had loved roses and now, every time she smelled them, Charlie pictured being cuddled up small in Nana's arms while she read her stories. All at once she grasped what Agatha meant.

"People c-can come back?" she asked in shock.

"No. Not really. Just their essence – their ghost, if you like. In magic we usually leave spirits be. But there are spells – dark spells that can summon them. And Samhain, when the veil between living and dead is weak . . . well, that's the perfect time to try."

"Zak said he wouldn't use spells on a *living* creature again. . ." said Kat slowly. "Do you really think he's going to call up a spirit?" Her green eyes were wide.

"I think he's going to try," said Agatha. "Zak is very confused at the moment. He's struggling with all kinds of things."

Charlie wanted to know more but Agatha had moved on. "The dark grimoire might have persuaded him that having a spirit familiar will bring him power." Agatha shook her head. "It's a very dangerous spell."

"There was a bright green light," Kat said quickly. "It swirled all around him."

Charlie nodded, "It kind of sc-scooped him up," she added.

"Havoc," Agatha said bluntly.

Charlie stared open-mouthed. So that was what havoc looked like!

"H-how do we stop him?"

Agatha sucked a breath through her teeth.

"You can't force Zak away from this path if he won't listen. He has to *want* to turn from dark magic. You'll never be able to drag him away yourselves." Her voice cracked. "I watched Eliza take the wrong road. I watched every month as she grew more and more haggard, more and more angry. I knew the havoc was coming but there was nothing I could do. She didn't want to try to get away from it. She didn't want to put the Book of Shadows down. She didn't want to change." Agatha sat down hard in her chair.

"There must be something we can do," said Kat.

Agatha leaned forward. "We do have one advantage," she said. A flare of hope rose in Charlie. "I didn't know when Eliza would cast her final curse. But, we know when Zak is most in danger. It's tomorrow night, at Samhain, under the eclipsed moon. That's the future you saw. We just need to work out where he'll go."

Charlie nodded slowly. She thought back to the

vision. "It was s-s-s-somewhere high," she began. "I think it was some kind of hill..."

"Yes," Kat joined in. "We were floating above it."

"There was a p-pattern in the earth, right in the gr-ground." Charlie turned the pages of her file and stopped at the pentagram, the five-sided star. "It looked kind of like this..." Her finger passed over it to the one below, a pentagram with a circle around it.

"The pentacle." Agatha nodded.

Kat gave a sudden cry. "Oh, I know!"

She pulled the book they'd taken from the library towards her – *A History of Broomwood*. She flicked hurriedly through until she found the page Zak had been looking at in the library. "There!" She pointed triumphantly to the page, which showed a slightly blurry aerial photograph of a field – with what Charlie could now see was a giant pentacle drawn into the earth.

Agatha drew in a sharp breath. "Broom Hill!" she whispered.

"Broom Hill?" Charlie had been there loads of times, but she'd never seen a shape like that.

"I'd forgotten!" said Agatha. "Long ago the old witch cottages were built on the points of a star," she said.

"You'd never know it from the ground – you have to be looking down from above to see it." She knelt next to Charlie and drew it out. "The plots were triangular, you see, and there was a meeting place in the middle, a stone Akelarre shaped like a pentagon. Round the edge was a wall, enclosing the star in a circle."

"That's wh-wh-what it looked like from ab-b-bove!" said Charlie in excitement. "Dad said they couldn't figure out why the c-c-c-cottages were triangular. Together they add up to m-make a star!"

"The pentacle brings great power," said Agatha. "It helps call spirits." Her face was pale.

"That's what he was looking up in the library," said Kat. "Where to find that shape!" She clapped her hands hard together once. "Now we know when and where he's casting the spell!" Then her face fell. "But so what?" She turned to Agatha. "You said we couldn't stop him, so what's the point?"

"We might not be able to stop Zak, but we could try to stop the havoc." Agatha was up and back to pacing again. She looked at her watch. "We have less than twenty-four hours." Her brow was furrowed in thought. "Is it even possible?" she spoke as if she was talking to herself.

"What? Is what p-p-possible?" Charlie pushed her.

"There is one way to stop havoc," said Agatha. "You have to soothe it, surround it with peace and calm. And for that you need a witch's ladder."

"A witch's ladder?" Kat repeated blankly.

"It's a kind of rope. But we don't have enough time. . ." Agatha fretted, tapping her fingers together quickly. She turned to her students. "You have to make the rope, you see. You make it out of vines and, as you weave it, you harness the energy of white magic. That's why it takes so long. As you make it, you focus on stillness and quiet; on nature, on love, on peace."

Something was tugging at Charlie's memory. "What . . . what does it l-l-look like, the witch's ladder?" she asked.

"It's a long rope," answered Agatha, "It has nine knots, each tied around a feather. You put markings on it, like this." She drew them out.

Charlie and Kat gasped in unison.

"We've seen one!" Kat cried.

"In Eliza's s-s-spell room!" said Charlie.

Agatha looked shocked. "Eliza?" she repeated. She clasped her hands together. Charlie could see her knuckles turn white as she gripped herself. "Eliza made a witch's ladder?"

"I think so," Kat nodded, "out of honeysuckle. It had feathers and bits of leaves in. It felt . . . good."

Tears filled Agatha's eyes. Her legs crumpled and Charlie grabbed her arm to stop her falling. She helped the witch to the chair. Agatha put her head in her hands.

Charlie didn't know what to say. She waited silently with Kat.

When Agatha finally lifted her head, her eyes were shining.

"This means Eliza wanted to change!" she said. "I'd always thought that she went to her death embracing dark magic, that there was no spark of goodness left in her. But that witch's ladder – it shows Eliza wasn't lost to dark forces. In her heart she must have been sorry for what she'd done to Suzy. She wanted to soften the havoc, to end it so she could return to white magic."

She gripped Charlie's hand.

"Get it!" she said. "Bring that witch's ladder here and we'll use it tomorrow night."

Chapter Eighteen

Trick or Treat

In the middle of the night, when everyone was asleep, Charlie opened the trapdoor under her fireplace and nervously made her way down the steps to Eliza's spell room.

At the bottom she tested the air for the horrible cold buzzing but, with the book gone, the room felt different. It was still dark and damp but the foreboding presence had disappeared. Charlie breathed out slowly. It was as though the room had relaxed somehow. She glanced around at all the old bottles and pots and jars, feeling the link with her great-aunt. She placed her torch sticking out of her pocket and picked up the witch's ladder.

It was lighter than it first looked. Long, but thin, the honeysuckle vine was an intricate weaving of dried herbs, leaves, stones and feathers. Charlie sniffed; after all those years it still carried a hint of lavender. She curled it up in her arms and gently carried it to her room.

In the light, Charlie could see the markings on the old wood: hundreds of sigils and wiggly shapes. It must have taken Eliza ages! She'd bring it over to Agatha's first thing in the morning.

She settled down in bed and tried to sleep. Her stomach felt all jumpy at the thought of what was to come. What if they couldn't help Zak? What was he planning to conjure up from the world of the undead?

She tossed and turned under her duvet. Just as she thought there was no hope of sleeping, the faint smell of lavender hit her. Her great-aunt's witch's ladder, made of honeysuckle for friendship, lavender for peace. She clung to what Agatha had said: Eliza hadn't been all bad. There was a way back for Zak, just as there had been for Charlie's great-aunt. Only this time, the lost witch would have support to bring him home.

*

Saturday morning was busy. In the kitchen Annie was sitting in her highchair, kicking her legs in excitement.

"Annie be a cat!" she reminded Charlie the moment Charlie came into the room.

"Yes I know!" said Charlie. "It's a very exciting day." She hugged her arms around herself to stop from bouncing up and down. The eclipse was due late tonight, at around ten p.m. That gave them only one day of training with the witch's ladder.

Mum was trying to get another bit of toast into Annie's mouth but Annie was far too wriggly. Mum wiped her hands on her dressing gown. "Are you and Kat still taking Annie trick or treating?"

"Definitely," said Charlie. "We're l-looking forward to it." Kat loved playing with Annie. She was an only child so for her it was a novelty having a three-year-old around. Plus it would be good to have something to do, something to occupy their minds other than the challenge ahead. "We'll come back and change into our costumes just before six."

"Annie be a cat!" Annie said again. Just to make sure everyone knew.

Charlie rushed out straight after breakfast, with

the witch's ladder in her backpack. Kat was waiting at the end of Charlie's garden, sitting on the wall.

"Did you get it?" she asked and Charlie nodded in answer, pointing her thumb at the bag on her shoulder. "Come on," said Kat, taking her hand. They ran through the narrow bushy path to Agatha's cottage.

Hopfoot was already there, sitting on Agatha's window sill, nibbling at nuts. He looked up and chirruped when he saw Kat.

"You look much better!" Kat cried and the crow nodded.

Charlie reached into her bag and took out the witch's ladder. "Here it is," she said and she handed it to Agatha. The witch uncurled it slowly, marvelling at all the work Eliza had put in.

"Oh, here is the sigil for love, and one for happiness . . . and . . . oh. . ." Agatha traced the loop design with her fingers. "One for friendship." Agatha had a faraway expression on her face. "Eliza didn't give up," she said to herself. She lifted her eyes to Charlie. "This rope might be able to help Eliza as well as Zak."

"What do you mean?"

"The witch's ladder is Eliza's last act of good. If we can use it to save Zak we can set her free from havoc, bring her spirit peace."

Charlie didn't understand.

"You'll see," said Agatha softly.

They practised over and over. Kat had to hold the rope – she needed to flip it through the air like a lasso.

"You have to surround the havoc," Agatha explained. "Really envelope it, then tie the rope tight." She demonstrated with a flick of her wrist. Kat copied her again and again. It was Charlie's job to control the havoc, pulling the icy wind together so Kat could throw the witch's ladder around it.

"It won't be easy," Agatha warned them. "Havoc is slippery: it will try to wriggle free of the rope. You have to be fast – fast and strong. The rope will charm the havoc, bewitch it into letting go. Then, Charlie, you'll need a chant to send it away."

Charlie felt ill at the thought of it. She swallowed hard. Agatha saw her struggling.

"You can do it." She held Charlie's face. "Remember what I told you; your voice is your asset.

It will force you to think about those letters more than anyone else. The trouble you have saying them will focus your mind, link you to the chant. Your voice will make you strong."

Charlie nodded and tried to believe her. She took out her notebook and began to write.

"Are you two ready?" Mum called up from downstairs.

"Nearly!" Charlie yelled back from her bedroom.

Charlie was just putting the finishing touches to her outfit. She was going as a pumpkin. She had a pair of Kat's stripy orange tights on her legs, and pillows stuffed down a bright orange jumper.

Kat wore a pair of fairy wings, a hot pink top and bright purple tights. Her hands fumbled as she pulled a bit of tinsel round her head.

"I can't believe that in four hours' time we'll be up on Broom Hill. A pumpkin and a fairy, armed with a rope made of honeysuckle."

Charlie grinned at her nervously, "Yeah. It does sound k-kind of stupid, when you p-put it that way."

Kat touched her hand and Charlie felt the hum of

their connection. "I know we can do it, Charlie. We can save Zak."

Charlie breathed in, sending the butterflies in her tummy away.

There was a knock at her door.

"I've got a little cat to see you," said Mum.

"Miaow," said Annie, peeping into the room shyly.

"Oh, it's a kitten," said Kat, moving to meet her. "How cute! I think it wants a saucer of milk."

Annie pulled on Kat's skirt, "It's Annie," she whispered to her. "No milk. Just sweets."

Mum laughed. "Not too many."

"Right," said Charlie. "Now I j-just need something green on my head, f-for the leaves. Then we c-can go."

"Use this," said Mum. She unwound Eliza's silk scarf from her neck.

"Perfect!" Charlie tied it round her head like a pirate bandana.

"I'm ready too," Matt was in the corridor, dressed all in black with a pointy hat on his head and a bright green face.

"Wa-ha-ha-ha!" he cackled at Annie and scooped her up.

"Can you have Annie back by eight please," said Mum.

"We *might* . . ." said Matt, ". . . or we *might* . . ." – he waggled his fingers in the air over his sister – "MIX HER IN A CAULDRON AND EAT HER UP!" he shouted, tickling her.

Annie squealed in delight.

Broomwood village was full of children in fancy dress. They walked up and down the streets carrying lanterns, glowsticks and bags full of sweets, celebrating Halloween night. Halloween, or All Hallows' Eve, was based on Samhain, Agatha had told them. In the olden days, on October the thirty-first, people dressed up as ghosts for protection: to trick evil spirits into thinking they were already dead.

Nowadays, the costumes were a little more varied. Through the darkness Charlie counted:

6 witches
3 cats
2 ghouls
3 fairies

4 Harry Potters
2 skeletons
2 ~~Spidermans~~ Spidermen
And 1 Buzz Lightyear

Annie hopped along between Kat and Charlie, lifting her feet to be swung every now and then. Matt was loudly practising his lines.

"*Fillet of a finny snake*," he was up to by the time they got to Wood Street.

Suzy Evans's house, in the shape of a castle, was strung with bright lanterns.

"Ooh, pretty!" said Annie as she looked at all the colours. Suzy was dressed as a fairy-tale princess, and she opened the door with an elegant curtsey.

"Hi, Charlie! Hi, Kat!" she sang out. Charlie smothered a grin. Suzy still had no idea that she and Kat were the reason her beautiful singing voice still worked.

"Hey, Suzy." Matt's voice was light, but he was blushing under his green paint. Charlie smirked. It looked like her brother had a little crush on someone! She made a mental note to tease him about it later.

By eight p.m. Annie was filled with as much

sugar as she could take and Kat and Charlie hoisted her up between them, giving her a ride home.

"Whee!" she cried as they ran all the way and deposited her, breathless, on the sofa.

"Thanks, girls," said Mum.

"That's OK," said Kat.

"We're g-g-going out again to watch the eclipse." Charlie pulled the stuffing out of her jumper and grabbed her coat. "It doesn't start till around ten p.m., so we'll be back late," she warned. A thread of excitement uncurled in her tummy.

"Be careful in the dark," said Mum as she wrestled a sweet out of Annie's hand.

"We will," Charlie promised. Well . . . apart from the bit where they'd try to make a load of havoc chill out, using an old rope.

Charlie pulled on her backpack, filled with everything they needed. She took Bess's scarf out of her hair to hand to Mum.

"No – keep it in case you get chilly," said Mum, yanking another sweet away from Annie. Charlie put the scarf in her coat pocket.

Kat took off her fairy wings. "You can have these, Annie!"

Annie grinned and clapped her hands.

"See you!" Kat called.

"Have fun!" said Mum, "No, Annie. I said no more sweets."

"Bye!" Charlie slammed the door. Then she looked at Kat. "Ready?"

"Ready," her familiar answered.

It was time.

Chapter Nineteen

Are You Ready for a Perfect Storm?

Up on Broom Hill, they waited.

They'd been there since nine o'clock, crouching behind a tree in the darkness. Charlie had a cramp in her leg and there was some kind of pine cone sticking into her side. She wriggled to free it and sent a rustle of leaves into the air.

Kat shushed her.

"When's he c-coming?" Charlie couldn't bear the waiting.

All day she'd been hoping that Zak would change his mind. All day she'd been anxious about their plan but, now that she was here, she just wanted to get it over with. She thought of Agatha, waiting back at the cottage by the fire. The witch stubbornly refused to do magic.

"My time has passed," she'd told Charlie. "I'm much better as a guide." Charlie knew that wasn't really true. Agatha had a strong force about her, an ability that had grown with years of experience. Every time she touched Charlie, the young witch felt it: a warm rush of power running through her veins. But tonight Agatha had refused to come.

"I'll wait here," she'd said calmly, her face full of confidence. "You don't need me."

Charlie was less sure. The plan felt a bit too vague – "calm" the havoc. What would it be like? How could a rope calm it? But, maddeningly, Agatha had just told her to follow her instincts. She glanced at her watch: nine-thirty p.m. The eclipse was due to begin soon. She looked up; there was a soft yellow moon in the sky, almost creamy. As she watched, a thin sliver of dark appeared as the earth began to move in front of the moon, blocking the sun's rays and putting the moon in shadow.

A cloud drifted overhead and the sky went dark.

Then, suddenly, there was a crunch of leaves and Kat stiffened beside her. Another crunch. Then another. Footsteps. Someone was coming. She heard the squelch of a foot into mud. The person was nearly here. She shrank back further.

Charlie peered into the blackness. She could just about see a figure moving, climbing up the last section of the hill. The cloud passed and the moving figure was instantly bathed in yellow light. Charlie bit her lip to stop herself making a noise.

It was Zak. Like in Kat's vision, Zak was covered in painted markings. It seemed like there were hundreds of odd shapes and symbols.

"Sigils," Kat whispered next to her. She was looking at them too.

Zak moved on, past the triangular-shaped pits and into the centre of the pentacle. He brushed away the mud from the stone in the middle. Then he lit five candles, one for every side of the stone pentacle, and put each one in place.

He knelt in the middle of the ancient stone and positioned something carefully in the centre. Charlie caught a glimpse of silver writing shining in the moonlight.

The other Book of Shadows!

Zak waited, gazing up at the moon.

From behind the tree, Charlie and Kat watched it too. Soon a curved line of shadow appeared at the edge of the creamy circle. The shadow grew, beginning to cover more and more of the moon. Still Zak waited. And waited. Charlie was about to scream with frustration when, just as the moon was nearly dark, Zak lifted his arms. In a deep voice he began to chant:

"WIND BLOW,
SPIRIT FREE.
I CALL TO YOU,
COME TO ME."

Charlie felt an icy chill course through her. The wind picked up. It whipped the leaves across the muddy ground, circling them round and round.

Zak called out again:

"I CALL TO YOU,
COME TO ME."

And Charlie could see a thin red light rise up out of the pentacle, as if someone had pointed a laser.

Zak remained motionless, staring ahead at the light.

There was a shift in the sky and Charlie looked up to see a blood-red moon. The total eclipse was here!

All at once the red light began to thicken. Before their eyes it bulged outwards. The shape of a long nose began to form, stretching towards Zak. It looked like a large animal, a huge beast, with bright red eyes and enormous claws.

Charlie gasped and clamped her hand over her mouth.

"Is that. . . Is that. . ?" Kat whispered in horror.

"I th-think it is," Charlie said in shock.

Zak hadn't summoned just any spirit. He'd summoned the spirit of a wolf – the Broomwood Wolf.

Charlie couldn't tear her eyes away from the red shape of the wolf. Her heart was thumping so hard in her chest she could feel it thudding against her ribs. She wasn't ready for this! She couldn't deal with a wolf! A wolf that, when living, had taken ten arrows to kill.

"I sh-should have realized that's what he was doing." She was furious with herself. She'd even spotted him with the book at the library. And he'd been hanging around the archaeological dig, so he would have heard all about the wolf – he'd probably even seen its bones.

"We both should have," Kat whispered back. "We just didn't put two and two together."

"What s-s-s-should we do?" Charlie fought the sudden desire to run away. Down the hill. Back to Agatha. Agatha would help. She'd know what to do.

Charlie felt Kat's warm hand touch hers. "It's just a spirit," the familiar said calmly. "The wolf is only a spirit. You can do this."

As they'd been talking, the red shape had grown. Now it towered over Zak . . . and . . . and . . . there was something else there too.

Charlie frowned and narrowed her eyes – it was another light. A thread of green silk grew up from the centre of the pentacle. As she watched, the thread began to dance. It hopped this way and that, curling and twisting its way, wrapping around the base of the wolf. There it was: havoc! Charlie's blood ran cold.

"Come to me,"

Zak called again.

"Come to me."

The thread worked its way up higher and higher until it had bound the red wolf in a plait of green. Under and over went the green thread until there was no more red visible. Havoc had taken over and the wolf was its puppet.

Charlie watched in horror as now the green thread inched its way across the sky from the wolf to Zak. It wrapped around his wrists, tight.

Zak's face went pale, as if it had been drained of blood.

"Ahhh" he cried. "Cold." He shook and wriggled to try to free himself of the thread.

But the green cord wrapped tighter, pulling him forward towards the bound wolf.

Zak cried out, as if in pain.

"Come on!" Charlie pulled Kat's hand.

They ran towards Zak, positioning themselves across from him at the edge of the pentacle.

Zak had his head down, struggling with the green cord that threatened to topple him over.

"Zak! Hold on! We're coming!" Kat yelled.

Zak lifted his head slightly. "What . . . are . . .

you . . . doing . . . here. . . ?" he gasped. He wobbled and the muscles in his arms tensed as he fought to remain upright.

"We're going to stop this," Charlie's voice rang out clear and true.

"No . . . no . . . I can do it," Zak grunted. He pulled back against the thread but the thread responded by yanking harder.

The havoc wolf opened its mouth. Panic gripped Charlie as the shape moved towards Zak.

"It's so cold," Zak winced. His face twisted.

Charlie closed her eyes. Quickly she caught Kat's thoughts. The familiar was sending her warmth. Charlie placed each foot firmly in the mud and stood up strong. She held her arms up and cried out her chant:

"Release your grip,
Let this boy go.
Free his arms,
Free his soul."

There was a howl of protest from the havoc wolf. It turned its icy green eyes on Charlie. All at once

Charlie felt a strong jolt run through her. Her head filled with the sound of bees. A sharp bitter scent rushed through her nose, stinging the inside of her throat as she breathed it in.

She set her jaw determinedly:

"Let this boy go."

She chanted again, keeping her voice still, focusing on every letter. She could feel Kat with her; their joined heat was pushing the cold wolf back. But the Broomwood Wolf was strong. Its bones had lain dormant for centuries, its spirit desperate to be free. Now the havoc was using its power for darkness.

Charlie struggled and the wolf grew larger.

Kat sensed her weakening.

"Zak!" she cried out. "Join us! You know how!"

In the centre of the pentacle, the boy hesitated for a moment. Charlie could see him choosing his path.

Zak's jaw tightened and he nodded. He had made up his mind. Charlie closed her eyes again and wished with all her heart that he had chosen well.

Chapter Twenty
Defying Gravity

Charlie felt a pushing in her mind. It was Zak. He was trying to get in.

"Let him through," Kat said in her head. Charlie paused, and then gave in – she had no choice but to trust him. She felt him, hesitant at first, uncertain of how to use white magic.

"You can do it," Charlie whispered to him in her head. Charlie could feel him trying to shake free of the cold darkness. "Come on, Zak. Fight it."

There was a short burst of strength from the boy.

"That's it!" Charlie cried as the heat hit her.

The three of them focused hard, and their

joint energy coursed to the centre of the stone, surrounding the cold green wolf with warmth.

It wasn't enough. All too soon Zak's strength gave out. He wasn't used to white magic, wasn't used to sharing his power. He didn't know how to harness his energy. The havoc wolf gave a howl of victory.

"No!" Charlie shouted. How could they teach Zak what to do? Her mind ticked over with ideas, filling her head and confusing her. *Stop*, she told herself. *Feel with your heart. What do you need*?

They needed more friendship, more connection, more love.

Charlie remembered the scarf. The green silk fabric in her pocket, worn by Eliza, and then her mother, and then Charlie herself. Family. Family was a tie no one could undo. Its bonds were stronger than anything. She pulled out the scarf. She threaded it through her fingers, the way she'd seen her mother do, and the silk slipped in and out. With her eyes still closed, Charlie tied the fabric in a knot. She pulled hard, concentrating on its warmth and history.

"Think of something happy!" she called to the others.

A vision of Hopfoot from Kat joined Eliza's scarf.

"I . . . I . . . can't. . ." Zak muttered.

"You can!" Charlie remembered his dream. "Think of how it feels to be an eagle, floating on the breeze, happy and free."

At her words Zak grew stronger. Charlie could feel him. He was an odd presence in her head. Kat was just Kat: she looked the same and sounded the same. But Zak, he twisted and turned inside her mind: now like a bird, now like a snake, now a mouse.

A wave of heat rushed up through Charlie as Zak's power grew.

She focused all the energy back towards the havoc wolf, enveloping the beast with warmth.

The wolf loosened its grip slightly.

"Let this boy go," Charlie shouted out.

There was a flash of white. A strong burst of heat . . .

. . . and the wolf released its claws!

Zak fell back, weakened but free. He scrambled out of the pentacle, towards the girls.

"Kat! Quick!" Charlie cried.

Kat swung the witch's ladder, round and round,

over her head. Then she let it fly. With her mind, Charlie helped direct it. It circled the wolf but, just as Charlie thought they had surrounded it, the rope loosened and the loop fell to the ground.

Something in the middle of the pentacle was giving the havoc power, stopping the witch's ladder taking hold.

Zak's Book of Shadows! It lay open, in the centre of the Akelarre, with jet-black pages and silver writing. The havoc wolf was tethered to its spine.

Kat turned her face away, "The glow. . ." she muttered. "It's so bright!"

Despair washed over Charlie. She could sense the cold power of the book even from back here.

Frantically, Charlie sought Kat's eyes. What should they do? They'd put Eliza's book to sleep, but now, with the wolf looming over them, they had no ingredients and no time to pick them. If only they could close the book, break the link – but there was no way any of them could go near that book. It was far too dangerous. . .

Suddenly Charlie knew what she had to do.

"I need your h-h-help!" she called to Zak and Kat

above the wind. "I'm going to use telekinesis to close the book!"

"What do I do?" Zak yelled back.

"Just follow what Kat does!" shouted Charlie. "Send me your energy!"

Before Charlie closed her eyes she took one last look at the face of the havoc wolf, suspended above the Book of Shadows in an icy mist. She shuddered and shut her eyes.

She focused all her energy on the book. A coldness swamped her, pulling her down, tempting her in. She almost took a step, reaching her hand out as if to touch it, but. . .

"No!" she heard Kat cry.

A moment later she felt the warmth of Kat and Zak. They harnessed the heat of the earth, tapping into the force of life, of nature. Charlie felt their power. The strength of it nearly lifted her into the air!

She pulled back from the cold, leaning into the force of warmth. She pictured the cover.

"Close! Close!" she muttered, her fists clenched tight.

She felt the leather give slightly.

"Close!" she cried again. The cover lifted. Charlie

could sense its heavy weight in her mind. She screwed her eyes tighter and pushed, pushed. Over it went and *snap*! It shut.

The green wolf was loose. It floated free, no book to tether it.

"Now, Kat!"

The familiar pulled Eliza's witch's ladder tight around the havoc wolf. The air around the wolf went hazy. Charlie felt a soft breeze wash through the cold night. It smelt of gentle lavender – calming, soothing. It charmed the havoc, bewitching the wolf and quelling the darkness. The havoc wolf swayed, hypnotised and stilled.

Charlie opened her mouth and let her voice call out, strong and clear:

"By blood-red moon,
By yellow sun,
I send you home,
I bid you gone."

The thread of green swirled in the sky as if it was circling a drain; then:

Whoosh!

The havoc was sucked down into the book, taking the wolf spirit with it. The rope fell to the ground.

Charlie ran forward and wrapped the Book of Shadows tightly in the witch's ladder. She covered it with Eliza's silk scarf. All at once a star shot down from the sky, streaking across the earth.

"Eliza!" Charlie whispered. "You did it!!"

She stumbled to the muddy ground, her knees weak with relief.

"Th . . . thanks." It was Zak. He slumped down next to Charlie and Kat. "I'm sorry. I thought I could do it . . . thought I could control the spirit." His face was pale and his hands trembled. "I don't know what came over me! I don't know why I did that spell. The book kept calling, taunting me to try it. . . I guess I'm not as strong as I thought."

"It's not your fault," Charlie said gently. "Th-that grimoire is very powerful. I was n-nearly tempted too."

"But you weren't."

"Only because I have Kat, and Agatha."

Zak gave a ragged sigh. "I think I should meet this Agatha."

"We'll take you to her," said Kat.

"Let me get my breath back first." Zak lay back on a patch of grass, stretching his hands up behind his head. Kat joined him and Charlie followed.

Together they gazed up at the blood-red moon. The air was cold and thin. It felt brittle, like glass, as if the world was fragile. Slowly a sliver of bright light began to appear at the edge of the moon, getting larger and larger as the moon moved out of shadow.

Charlie felt a hum of warm energy run through her as the moon's light grew stronger. Next to her, Zak wriggled.

"Did you feel that?" he asked.

Charlie grinned and nodded. The chaos had passed. That sense of spinning, of discord and uncertainty, was gone. A calmness washed over her and she reached for Kat's hand. Kat squeezed in answer and Charlie closed her eyes, enjoying the moment of peace.

There on the grass, the friends lay, still and silent like sentinels, watching till the moon was full and yellow once again.

Chapter Twenty-One

Blessed Be

"I didn't know magic could feel like that," Zak was saying.

They were sitting in Agatha's cottage, mugs of nettle tea on their laps.

"I thought it was always cold and painful," he winced, "but your magic," he looked from witch to familiar, "it was warm and soft."

"White magic," Agatha answered briskly. Her words were abrupt but her tone was gentle.

Zak hung his head. "I'm sorry," he said. "I'm so sorry about everything." He blushed as he looked at Hopfoot. The crow was much better now. He sat on Agatha's window sill listening to Zak. Zak turned to Agatha to explain.

"At first I just wanted friends. I wanted to be popular. But then, when I met Charlie and Kat, I realized it was more than that." He put his mug down, eager to explain. "I was jealous of what they had." He looked down at his hands and shrugged. "I've always been able to make things happen, little things, but I've always sensed there was part of me that wasn't right, that didn't fit in with the rest of me. . ." He struggled to say it. "Like a bit of me was out of control."

"I see that," Agatha said drily.

"When I met Kat I thought . . . I thought I just needed someone like her, a familiar, then that part of me would be fixed." He ran his fingers through his hair. "Ah, this isn't making any sense at all!"

"It is to me," said Agatha. She put another log on the fire. It hissed and spat. She turned to Zak. "You're a shape-shifter," she said bluntly.

A thrill ran down Charlie's spine. Yes! The second Agatha said it, everything fell into place.

"A what?"

"A shape-shifter. My great-great grandmother was one. It means you can change into an animal."

Charlie was always amazed at how matter-of-factly Agatha spoke of these things.

"But I can't." Zak shook his head in disbelief. "I have dreams about turning into animals – but that's all. I can't actually do it."

"Well, no. Not yet you can't!" Agatha gave a little laugh. "You'd have to train for a long time before you could. But you have the signs of a shifter now. It's why there's a part of you that's different; it's how you managed to possess Hopfoot" – Zak looked embarrassed – "and why, of all the spirits available, you didn't summon a human spirit; you summoned a wolf. The Broomwood Wolf."

There was a silence. Then Zak spoke again:

"Sometimes I have these visions," he admitted. "I see the earth below me as if I'm flying, or the grass above me as if I'm tiny."

Agatha nodded. "You can learn to control them," she said. "Learn to harness their power."

Zak shook his head again slowly.

"But for now" – Agatha passed Zak a pile of honeysuckle – "you can help us see the new year in."

There was a pause and then, with a grin, Zak began to weave his blessing wreath.

*

By the early hours of the new year the four wreaths were ready to hang. The witches placed them high on the branches of the trees surrounding the cottage.

Then they closed their eyes and thought of the old year that had passed, and the new year to come. The two Books of Shadows, the grimoires of the Snake Sisters, were locked away now, sealed inside Agatha's iron chest. The one Zak had used was still bound in Eliza's rope. Charlie had watched Agatha give the witch's ladder one last stroke, passing her fingers over the honeysuckle and stopping at the loop sigil, the symbol of friendship. Agatha had given a little smile. Gently, she'd untwined the twig holding the sigil and plaited it into her own Samhain wreath. Then Agatha had wrapped the grimoire in an extra layer of mulberry silk, and locked it in the chest.

Charlie felt lighter inside, almost dizzy with happiness. The connection with her great-aunt tingled through her body, soft and warm. Before she'd died Eliza had tried to turn back to white magic – she'd tried to save her friendship with Agatha. And, all these years later, by helping Charlie, Eliza had managed to restore it. She was finally at peace.

"Do you have the blessing chant ready, Charlie?" Agatha asked.

Charlie nodded. She was ready.

She handed each person a candle. She closed her eyes and reached for her two friends' hands. She could feel the energy run into her, from the familiar on one side, and the shifter on the other.

In her clear, strong voice she chanted:

"By fire hot,
By night-time cold,
We think of friends
Both new and old.
We bless this land
And people here,
We bring them strength:
New start, new Year."

"And what do you want to achieve this year, Charlie?" Agatha asked her as they said goodbye.

"I'm g-going to fix up Eliza's spell room," she said firmly. She had been thinking about this for days, and now she was sure. "I want to learn to sp-spellcast properly and it's going to be v-very useful getting in and out of it via my own fireplace."

"I'll help!" said Kat.

"Me too," said Zak shyly, "If you'll let me."

"We'll let you." Charlie smiled at him. "We n-need someone to do the d-dirty work."

"*Thanks*," said Zak sarcastically. "Anyway, by then I'll have probably managed to shape-shift into a fox or something. So I'll be able to sweep up all the mess with my bushy tail." He raised his eyebrows at Agatha, who shook her head *"No you won't"*. Her eyes twinkled though, so Charlie could tell she was secretly amused.

On Monday night the family gathered together to see Matt in the school's production of *Macbeth*.

They shuffled into their seats in the auditorium. Charlie sat next to Annie and saved the two seats on her other side for Kat and Zak.

"Here!" she whispered, waving to her friends as the lights went down. Kat slipped in beside her and Zak grabbed the last seat on the aisle.

"Who's got the toffees?" said Dad from down the row.

"Shush, Nick," said Mum. "It's starting."

"I only want a toffee," Dad grumbled.

"Here, Daddy!" said Annie loudly. She pulled a sweet from her mouth and passed it down the line to Dad.

"Er. Great. Thanks, Annie," Dad whispered.

Kat giggled.

The curtain squeaked back on the school stage. There was a flash of light and three witches shuffled on to the stage wearing tall black hats, cloaks and green face paint.

"*Double, double toil and trouble, Fire burn, and cauldron bubble.*"

They cackled in unison.

Annie's eyes were wide. "Witches, Charlie!" she whispered, as she pointed at the stage.

"Kind of," Charlie answered, and she smiled to herself.

They were nothing like the ones Charlie knew.

Abie Longstaff has written many successful picture books, including *The Mummy Shop* and *Just the Job for Dad*, as well as the *Fairytale Hairdresser* series. Her books for older children include *The Magic Potions Shop* and *The Trapdoor Mysteries*. Abie lives in Hove with her family.